AUTUMNGALE

BRIDGE OF LEGENDS

BOOK THREE

SARAH K. L. WILSON

This is a work of fiction. All characters, places, and events are purely fictitious.

AUTUMNGALE

ISBN: 978-0-9878502-9-4

Cover art by POLAR ENGINE

Map by Francesca Baerald

Appendix art by Harold Trammel

www.sarahklwilson.com

Direct comments or feedback to sarah@sarahklwilson.com.

For Cale

Always

Legends

Byron Bronzebow

A good-looking hero who carries a bronze bow. Known in history for his care for the poor and needy.

Deathless Pirate

Known for his love of treasure and invulnerability and recognized by his hook for a hand and belt of human skulls.

Grandfather Timeless

Based in the Timekeepers religion he is known for his high hat, long black coat and golden waistcoat. He is Time in human form subjecting all to his will.

King Abelmeyer the One-Eyed

Known for his single eye and broken crown, King Abelmeyer united the five cities of the Dragonblood Plains in the alliance that lasts today.

Lady Sacrifice

Known for her loveliness, innocence and sacrifice for the people, she is usually clad in a white dress.

LILA CHERRYLOCKS

A master thief and trickster. Known for her long cherry-red locks, deft skills, and adventurous spirit.

MAID CHAOS

The right hand of Death. Known for destruction, death and the golden breastplate she wears.

QUEEN MER

Queen of the Sea and mother to the Waverunners. Queen Mer is known for her revenge upon man in the form of hurricanes and typhoons and for the shells, scales, and seaweed that she wears.

RAM THE HUNTER

The unspoken Legend. Not mentioned in the Dragonblood Plains except in whispers, he is known for slaying dragons and going insane in the aftermath.

BRIDGE OF LEGENDS
JINGEN
Districts
Alchemist
Governement
Temple
University
Spire
Artificier
Trade

Prologue

"And in those days brother fought against brother and father against son as the factions fought for control of the cities until one voice rose up and calmed them all. One voice could be heard ringing out over the people – the voice of Mer. And she became our Queen, the savior of our lives."

– *Legends of the Dragonblooded*

"The Ancient Legends, bane of man, riders of dragons, Emperors of sky and stars – they had to be stopped. They had to be contained. We were willing to give anything to stop them – our blood, our bones, our children."

– *Ancient text found on a scrap of parchment from the Time Before.*

"And the voices called to him. And the pillars of the earth shook. And sanity found no place in the world beyond. For the Legends were reborn and their fate overtook them. The ancient ones rose again, the skies burned and the water was licked up before them. And they named him death – the stealer of life, the murderer of hope the destruction of our souls.

– *Songs of the Retribution*

1: Burning City

TAMERLAN

Tamerlan clutched Abelmeyer's Eye to his chest, his own single eye studying Etienne's face as Jhinn steered their gondola out of H'yi to the Cerulean river. The other man was sober – grim in the flickering light and shadows of the dying flames.

The clock still stood – unaffected by the fires – prison, sanctuary, and trap. And back there at the heart of H'yi, in its depths, Marielle flickered in and out of life – a half-living ghost.

Tamerlan choked down what he thought might be a sob. This wasn't a time for tears. And what Marielle needed right now wasn't a tearful boy. She needed a tragedy-hardened man ready to fight for her.

He coughed on the smoke clouds they drifted through – relieved it was only the smoke of a burning city and not the smoke that altered everything.

Black clouds surrounded them, blocking out the drifting boats of survivors coughing and hacking on the choked rivers. He thought he saw a man collapse in a boat further down the river – saw the others in his boat scrambling to his aid. It was hard to tell in all the smoke and chaos. There would be more deaths as people fled. There was too much smoke to get a clean breath.

This was a time to face grim reality, though his single eye wasn't ready to face anything.

He'd made a choice back on Summernight to save Marielle and doom everyone else, and he'd been watching the horrific consequences of that choice play out ever since. When he had the same choice to make all over again on Dawnspell, he'd tried to find redemption by choosing the other option – dooming her to save everyone. It should have felt like he'd done the right thing. It should have felt like redemption.

Instead, it was ashes and bitterness in his mouth.

Whatever he did now would have to be different. It would have to heal and not destroy. He would have to find some third option.

He coughed on the billowing smoke, leaning down to wet his neck scarf in the river water to tie around his nose and mouth like Etienne had. It took two tries to gauge his swipe at the water correctly. It was going to take time to get used to losing vision in one eye.

Smoke seemed fitting. It was as opaque as his situation. It choked out life just like his decisions did. It felt as insubstantial as his demons.

He needed guidance.

The world spun as he tried to adjust to his one working eye. He blinked, trying to clear his vision. It would never be fully clear again. And even that didn't seem like full payment for all he'd done. If he hadn't asked Marielle to scent for him, she wouldn't be in the clock.

And the dragon would still rage across the earth, Abelmeyer reminded him. He was still there – still haunting Tamerlan's mind.

And your pretty behind would be as dead as everything else on the Dragonblood Plains. That was Lila haunting him, too.

"We'll get her out," Etienne said, looking at the clock in the distance. Soon, the sight of it would be lost in the smoke. His hands were shaking. And no wonder. His crimes were as full and deep as Tamerlan's now. Without him, the Legend Grandfather Timeless would still be in the clock. And Marielle would not be.

"Promise me," Tamerlan said through gritted teeth. Redemption wasn't possible anymore. Forgiveness was not something he'd ever taste. But he could at least be faithful in this one thing. "Promise me that you will not rest until she's out of the clock – that you'll work with me to free her."

Etienne looked up at the clouds of black smoke swirling above them. "There are things – plans – things I need to do to help my people."

"You're the one who freed the Legend," Tamerlan said through gritted teeth. "You opened the Bridge of Legends and let him out."

Etienne looked back at him, fury in his eyes. "With that recipe of yours. With that mixture of yours. One breath of smoke and he took me completely – held me for days to do his bidding. Is that your magic, Tamerlan? Possession by spirits?"

"Not spirits," Tamerlan said, tightly. "Legends. And I can control it."

Etienne's laugh was harsh. "No one can control it, Tamerlan. It controls you. It's an evil thing. A thing that should not be touched."

He stole magic from the dragon, day after day – that's where his power came from before you took it from him. That didn't seem to trouble him, but one brush with the Grandfather and he's done with magic? Lila sounded disbelieving. *Hypocrite.*

Dragon. Dragon. Dragon. Even with the dragon stopped, Ram was still just an insane echo constantly ranting in the back of Tamerlan's mind.

"Like the magic you siphoned from the dragon before he fled?" Tamerlan asked.

"Dragon's spit! It's not the same. It was never for me."

"Neither was this!"

"It was always for the good of others."

Tamerlan's replies were getting louder. "What did you think this was for?"

"Chasing goals for yourself is easy. Trying to do good for a whole population is a lot harder!"

"Do you think it was easy to go against a whole city to save my sister? Did you think it was easy to halt a dragon in the sky? Do you think it's easy to lose an eye? Oh, it's still there – but it doesn't see. I gave that up to stop him – to stop you."

Etienne looked away but Tamerlan couldn't stop. He felt like all his edges were raw.

"And Marielle is in a clock. And the world is still falling apart!"

And he didn't see a way clear. Didn't see any reason to keep going when all was lost. Except maybe for her.

"You have to stop smoking that stuff," Etienne said quietly. He looked stoic and dignified as he watched the horizon before them. "It's a magic you don't understand and can't control."

"I'll stop when it's over. When everything is right again." Because how else would he fix it? He couldn't do it on his own – he never could.

Lean into us, Alchemist. We can help you. You don't need to do it alone. Lila's words were as enticing as honey.

"It will never be over," Etienne said with a shudder. "One thing only leads to another. Always. Forever."

"Then what's the point? What's the point of anything?" Tamerlan asked and his words hung in the air like the black smoke above them – just as choking and grim.

"Adventure," Jhinn said from the back of the boat. Tamerlan had almost forgotten he was there. "It's all we're promised in life – an adventure."

If only life could be so simple.

"I promise," Etienne said, heavily. "I make my vow to you as Etienne Velendark, formerly the Lord Mythos of Jingen that I will not rest until Marielle Valenspear is out of the clock. I will work with you to accomplish this."

He leaned forward and seized Tamerlan's hand. Tamerlan flinched back from a searing heat like fire bursting up his arm. Pain reverberated through him as he tried to pull his hand back. Etienne held it firmly in place, a smile of smug satisfaction on his face.

"I have at least enough power left to do that. We're bound now, you and I. Dragon help me, but we're bound."

"If we're bound then we'll find Grandfather Timeless," Tamerlan said. "We'll bind his avatar again. And we'll get Marielle out of the clock. We owe it to her. She's the only one of us without blood on her hands."

They broke their handclasp, each looking out over the fiery horizon. Each consumed by his own demons as they made their way up the river, looking for any sign of the Legend they were promise-bound to hunt.

And in the clock, Marielle slept – or didn't sleep – as time ticked on.

And under the thick, fecund mud of the Dragonblood Plains, the dragons slept – and dreamed – and drew closer to the world of man.

Drawing Bounds

Night One of Autumngale

Two Months Later

2: Rain on the River

Tamerlan

"Those books are going to get wet, boy," Jhinn said as Tamerlan held his book out from the edge of the tarp, trying to read in the flickering light of the gondola lamp.

"There has to be an answer in here. What is he trying to accomplish? Where is he going?"

"Where does the wind go? What does it want?"

"Maybe there's a way to trap him. Some way to keep him from slipping through our fingers again."

Jhinn snorted as he worked his wrench. "You want to trap time? Good luck with that. You know what your Lord Mythos says about that. He says your only chance is to surprise him."

They had pulled the gondola under the edge of a bridge as the torrent poured down on them and Tamerlan had the tarp pulled over his head as he read, trying to keep the precious books dry, but even with so many precautions it was hard to read without getting raindrops smeared across the ink of the pages.

"Etienne doesn't know everything," he muttered.

The *drip, drip, drip* was a near-constant thing, and the sound of rain on water – while soothing – blocked out everything from the world around them so that it seemed like it was only them and the boat and the bridge and the rain.

"Lord Mythos isn't going to be happy if he comes to life again and sees you've wrecked his books. He told you they were hard to get. He bribed a Librarian to get them. What do you think he bribed her with? He doesn't look like one to kiss in corners or take a girl down to see the falls."

Tamerlan's smile quirked up in one corner of his mouth. Jhinn's firm belief that anyone not on the water was not real – or was at the very least dead – constantly fascinated him. Waverunner beliefs were simple enough to grasp, but hard to really understand. Or maybe it was just the absolute conviction of those beliefs that was hard to believe. Tamerlan didn't know anything for sure anymore.

Right now he couldn't be distracted by that. Etienne had visited the gondola that morning with a new book – the sixth one he'd brought from the Bronzebow Library all the way in Xin. Half the reason they hadn't caught Grandfather Timeless yet was all these trips of Etienne's all over the Dragonblood Plains. If he would just stay in Yan with them, they'd be able to search together. Like the other books, he claimed it would have new information they could use to trap Grandfather Timeless.

The Grandfather will not be easily trapped. And certainly not by anything found in a book.

That might have been Lila Cherrylocks. Or maybe Byron Bronzebow. Or maybe it was Tamerlan's own thoughts. He was having trouble keeping them apart after all these months – not that they didn't sound different from one another. Their voices simply flowed through his thoughts so constantly that he was barely conscious of them most of the time, speaking into his mind and into his dreams, making judgments, fueling ambitions, but always talking, talking, talking and never giving him a moment of peace. He'd pay all these books and the cloak on his back for just one precious moment of peace.

His hands shook as he turned a page, reading intently and ignoring Jhinn's chastisements. It was getting harder not to smoke when he didn't need to. There was a relief in hearing just one voice instead of all of them. It didn't help that his brain felt sluggish when he wasn't smoking the spices. He'd started thinking of them just as "Spices" because it made it easier to smoke than when he admitted what he was doing – that he was accessing an ancient, deadly magic that no one should touch.

"If you're going to ignore warnings, at least tell me what you think I should do now that I've fitted the gears together. Is this looking good to you?" Jhinn asked, pointing at his latest creation.

Tamerlan looked up at the device Jhinn was building for his gondola. He'd been working on it for weeks now, slowly making one part after another and always casually asking what Tamerlan thought of it each time. It was growing so large that it was hard for it to fit easily in the gondola with both of them and all the books and the makeshift tent and cookpot, too. The gondola was looking more and more like a family boat all the time.

"It looks good," Tamerlan said absently. His mind was still working on what he'd just read, and he was barely paying attention as he said, "Maybe add a belt that moves between two pulleys attached to that gear there and that one there. That would mean you could drive the new gear from the motion of the rotary action over here."

He paused. What had made him say that? But Jhinn was just smiling and nodding encouragingly.

"Good, good," he said before choosing a wrench from his leather bag and getting back to work.

Tamerlan shook his head. Sometimes it felt like his mind – even his mouth – weren't his own anymore. It was disconcerting but he'd be more concerned about it if he didn't have so much already bothering him. He looked back down at the book and at the corner where his hand had been idly sketching with the sharp charcoal Etienne had found for him. He shouldn't be marking up books. Especially not library books in the rain with a tarp spread over him like a child under the covers.

But there in black and white was her face. Again.

Marielle.

He thought about her so constantly that he drew her face without thinking. He dreamt of her every night. Longing, anguished dreams.

Last night he'd watched her fleeing from an army, only to turn into a tree to hide. The army had lit the tree on fire and the cracks and pops as it burned sounded like her screaming.

Was his obsession with her guilt or was attachment? Or was it something else entirely? He didn't even know anymore. All he knew was that he needed to get her out.

Two months and she was still in the clock.

Two months and he still hadn't caught the Legend who put her there – the Grandfather. Even the voices in his head were growing dumbfounded. Every time he was close, the Grandfather slipped away into the shadows.

They'd chased him from tavern to inn to temple in each of the remaining four cities. And they were no closer to catching him now than they'd been when they left the choking smoke of H'yi.

It was hard to chase the Grandfather. They'd lose his trail for weeks, only to suddenly catch wind of him somewhere. Wherever he was caused a flurry of activity among the Timekeepers – his priests – and that was their only hint most of the time. But they'd arrived at the Sun of Light Temple in Xin last time, only to find it empty and a single Timekeeper priest left to stare blankly as they asked their questions.

That was when Etienne had decided to turn to Yan.

"We haven't tried there yet," was his weak reasoning.

Tamerlan blinked, his single working eye squinting at the text again. Maybe this time there would be a key in the book. Someone had to know something about how Grandfather Timeless worked. Someone had to have known him before he was a Legend.

His single eye slid along the line of words and he fought against the irrational fear that one eye meant he was missing something – not seeing something right there. He worried that maybe he'd breezed over something because his single eye was too tired – something important.

He blinked and read the last sentence again.

"For what can stop time? No mortal or Legend can quell the passing of the years or the ravaging of them. For what we build up, time tears down. What we birth, time ages. What we delight in is no more and even the ashes of it fade away. But seize wisdom and learn from understanding. Let it open your eyes to truth and let all your paths be guided by it. Look, wisdom opens the gate and understanding the mountain. Look, they have buried insight under the waters and prudence under the rocks."

He sighed. This whole book read like that. Sure, it talked about time. And yes, he loved to read this kind of text when he wasn't desperate for answers. He loved to think about wisdom and philosophy and dream about what could be. But right now, this was worse than useless. There was no key here for trapping the Grandfather. And he was going to have to figure out a trap of some kind. All this stalking and hunting wasn't doing anything. He was always a dozen steps ahead of them.

Tamerlan opened the other book – the one that kept worrying him but that he kept returning to, over and over, again and again. It was a book entitled *Prophecies of the Latter Legends* and it spoke in a complicated, vague way that should have annoyed him and yet he resonated with it.

"Beware the Howling Dark. The last remains of the shell of humanity, the last derelict flesh of the forgotten mind. Beware when it steals your voice and covers your desires. Beware when it howls, ever echoing down the chambers of the mind until all is forgotten but dusk and dust. Beware. For many have tried but few have succeeded. Many have crossed the final bridge only to discover there is no way back and that they left themselves on the far side of that great river which is death."

The Howling Dark worried him. It sounded a bit too much like his mind now that the Legends had taken it over. He turned a page, ignoring the drip of the rain and the click of Jhinn's tools and the rising scent of algae and water lilies as the rain teased it out.

"Do you think we can trap him, Jhinn? How do you trap a Legend?"

"How did they trap Deathless Pirate?"

Tamerlan shivered, thinking back to when they'd seen his avatar floating under the ocean in a metal cage. "I don't know, but however they did it, it wasn't very nice."

Jhinn shrugged. "Then your solution won't be very nice. Do you think it needs a device? Like the clock? I could try making a clock when I'm done with this gondola."

A loud thump brought Tamerlan's head up in time to see Etienne land on the boat. He'd jumped from the bridge above, rain soaking his cloak and dripping dark hair. The half-light of a stormy day drew his face in stark, haggard lines – he always looked haggard now, more with every snatch of news they received in every city. Tamerlan would have almost felt sorry for him except that the worn look of guilt on his face was deserved. They were brothers in shame. Partners in crime. Twins in unabsolved sin.

"You're not drawing in the margins again?" Etienne asked, snatching the book from Tamerlan's hands. "Her again! Always her. Clear your mind, Alchemist! You won't find the Grandfather when you're daydreaming." He threw the book back at Tamerlan and Tamerlan barely caught it.

"I have a lead – a hint of where we can find our quarry," Etienne said grimly. "Strap on your sword and let's go."

"Right now?" Tamerlan blinked in surprise as he carefully wrapped the books back up in oilcloth to protect them.

"You want to wait? You haven't done enough waiting?" He was on edge, his eyes firing and his words snapping out like whips.

Tamerlan looked around them at the boats huddled together under the bridge in the rain – it was easy to forget they were there when the rain muffled the sounds from boat to boat.

Everyone minded their own business in these moments. They were forced together by weather and geography. No need to make more of it than it was. And yet there was anonymity in numbers. In daylight, moving in the canals would bring notice.

"Waiting is better than being caught by the Harbingers," Tamerlan said. "I'm telling you, they're following us. I swear I saw the woman – Liandari? – when I was in the market yesterday. Her eyes are sharp." It had definitely been her. He'd barely given her the slip once she'd caught sight of him.

"You worry too much about them," Etienne said. But he looked worried, too. It was hard enough to be hunters without being the hunted, too. And at their last stop, the innkeeper had mentioned someone was looking for them – someone with a sharp sword and coin to spend on information. "We need to go before we lose the trail again. Who knows how long he'll stay this time?"

And that was as true as breathing.

"What will we do when we find him?" Tamerlan asked as he strapped his swords on. "He'll only slip away again. We need some kind of trap."

He slipped his rolls of Spices into his sleeve and tried not to think about all the times that the Legend had given them the slip. It was hard to find and catch a Legend. It was worse when he wasn't bound by time like they were.

"This time will be different," Etienne muttered. "We don't have a trap. We don't have any allies. All we have is surprise."

Different, Different. Different.

The voices in Tamerlan's head were in unison this time. They wanted this too. Or maybe that was him. He couldn't tell one from another anymore. His hands shook in anticipation.

This time, he'd be ready. This time, he'd catch the Grandfather, no matter what he had to do.

3: Inside the Clock

Marielle

The tick of the universe was in her ears – always.

It wasn't that she hadn't been watching or that she hadn't seen. It was that she was seeing everything, all the time.

Because she was time and when you are time, everything is always happening at once inside you – the roll of the seasons as seen from the stars. The life of a man as seen by the burning cosmos. The rise and fall of generations as seen by the mountains looming above.

Everything.

All the time.

It wasn't that she wasn't seeing what was happening to her friends. It was just that it was hard to pick out what was happening *now* instead of thirty years ago. Or thirty years from now. And that made her head ache because the future was blurry – like watching the same person overlaid on a scene a hundred different times and all one hundred of that person were doing slightly different things – or vastly different things. When you were talking about hundreds of variations, it went from incremental to enormous in the blink of an eye.

And that was what she'd been doing.

She'd been blinking.

And with every blink, she tried to get closer to the time when she'd been put in the clock.

To now.

To Marielle.

And what if she was too late – if she forgot who she was? She didn't dare think about that.

4: THE WHISPER

TAMERLAN

Yan City was laid out just like Jingen and Xin had been. Just like H'yi. Just like every city of the Dragonblood Plains. But just like the other cities, it had subtleties of its own. Here, the canals were wider and slower moving. Here there were more oxen pulling carts and more people jammed into the streets. Buildings were higher and more crowded and the people in Yan had an obsession with carefully wrought lanterns and woven rugs. They could be seen hanging in any space available or layered one upon the other on the floors of their dwellings. Hawkers sold them faster than hotcakes on the streets. Surely, everyone must have as many as they could afford. And yet more were being sold all the time.

Tamerlan's single eye scanned the streets, taking in the sellers of chalk hiding under canopies as the rain poured down. Chalk was an important part of the week-long Autumngale Festival. But getting it wet wouldn't help anything. And who was going to buy it in Yan City where everyone watched the world with hollow eyes?

"Chalk for the festival? Chalk to win the city?" a hawker cried, holding up a stick of chalk as fat as Tamerlan's thumb.

One of them looked his way and then quickly looked away again. Tamerlan laughed internally. No, he and Etienne did not look like chalk buyers, did they?

He glanced at the other man. As usual, Etienne strode through the city like he owned the place, waving off hawkers like servants. But looking like you owned a place and actually owning it, were two entirely different things.

"News from Xin City," a crier yelled. "A penny and I will tell you how it has been rebuilt after the fires. Two, and I'll tell you who holds power there now!"

Etienne waved him off irritably. Etienne probably knew better than the newscrier anyway. He visited Xin City often – and always without Tamerlan. It was one of many reasons why their hunt for the Grandfather had been delayed.

The crier tried a last attempt as they melted into the crowd. "Five pennies and I'll tell you why H'yi burned to the ground while Xin still stands!"

Like they needed to know. They'd seen the firs themselves. Comparing Xin to H'yi was like comparing a candle to a campfire.

A child hid from the rain against a stone wall as they passed, his clothing ragged, his cheeks gaunt. The huddle of cloth behind him could be a mother, given up hope after being a refugee for months. Or it could be a child seller. Or a dead man. It was impossible to know. So many orphans in the cities now, and so many belonging to families too poor to feed and clothe them – and all of them needed more than Tamerlan could give. Though he tried to help where he could.

He pressed a pair of coins into the child's hand, sinking to his knee for a moment to whisper, "Get something hot to eat, hmmm?"

The child's gap-toothed grin made his heart lurch. The boy needed more than a couple of coins. When all this was done and the Grandfather was dealt with, Tamerlan was going to start an orphanage. A place for children who needed more help than a coin could give.

He hurried to catch up to Etienne who caught his eye before raising a single brow. He didn't hand out coins on the street.

"You only draw attention that way," he said gruffly – repeating what he said last time. "Better to have given the coins to the newscrier."

Tamerlan ignored him. Maybe they'd never catch the Grandfather. Maybe they'd never save the cities. But they could do this good thing right now. So, why not do it?

"News! Hear ye all!" a second crier said from the street corner. Here in Yan, they dressed in red so they could be seen easily. If only it were easier to ignore them. They were thick as flies on the troubled city and they never said anything Tamerlan wished they would say. "Lord Fable has declared this year the Year of the Cantonelles! Cantonelle players will be here to play in every inn and city square throughout the Festival!"

Tamerlan clenched his jaw. Cantonelles. They played cantonelles in his home Landhold. They were his father's favorite music. More evidence of Decebal's growing hold in Yan showed up on the streets every day and every day Tamerlan clenched his fists tighter and pressed his lips more closely together.

"Dragon cursed cantonelles," he muttered, but he was distracted. Yan was not a happy city. If his father would stop maneuvering and actually use his power for something good, he could do something about that.

Lines of refugees filled the streets, choking the pathways even here in the Temple District. The palace was offering a daily dole of bread and soup – but only once a day and only to those who agreed to live outside the city walls. They were marked with woven bands of leather around their heads. Anyone wearing the band could receive the dole. And anyone wearing the band wasn't welcome within the city walls after dark.

Despite the lash of the harsh autumn rain, people waited in long hollow-eyed lines.

And with every look they shot at Tamerlan he shivered. He didn't have enough coins for all of them. Not even for all the children. Glimpses of them tore his heart to shreds. This wasn't how they were meant to live. But he was the one who took their homes and stability. He needed to smoke and forget again.

Yes! Forget again! We wait for you. That was Lila Cherrylocks. She sounded hungrier every time she spoke now. And he was sure she was holding out on him – waiting until he caved and smoked again.

And yet he didn't dare do that. The last time he'd smoked, he'd lost the vision of his eye. And with every day that passed without a puff of the Spice, his hands shook more wildly and the voices grew louder.

Why didn't Etienne's hands shake? Was it because he only smoked once?

Or is it because Grandfather Time went free? His body doesn't crave the return of a Legend who can't come back to it anymore, Lila suggested. *Which is why it can't hurt you if you only call up the Legends you've called before.*

An interesting theory. But Tamerlan had no control over which Legends came over the Bridge.

I'm an interesting person.

Half the time he didn't know if Lila was flirting with him or just being herself.

Both. Of course.

Tamerlan couldn't look anymore at the small children in line, clinging to adult hands with hollow eyes. Children shouldn't have to bear the debt of their elders.

He tried to focus on where he and Etienne were going instead. They were nearly in the Temple District. He could see the spires of the Timekeeper's temples and cathedrals up ahead. The Smudgers wouldn't be there. They had not returned since the day Tamerlan had released Jingen and they'd fled to the hills north of the Five Cities.

He glanced at one of their temples. Brazier holders were empty outside the gate. People had stolen the bronze bowls from the holders and the way the door hung ajar suggested that the inside had been raided, too.

We'll help the children tonight, Byron Bronzebow promised. *This time, you'll call me, and we'll do it right.*

Tamerlan's hand shook as he felt the oil-cloth package in his pocket – the rolls of Spices just waiting to be smoked. Maybe this time he really would call Byron Bronzebow. He and Etienne tried to help the refugees every night – but two people could only do so much. Maybe it wouldn't be the worst thing to call on a Legend to help.

He swallowed, his mouth dry at the thought.

It would be wise. A good idea.

Or maybe not.

He pulled his hand back from his pocket. He felt eyes on the back of his neck, but when he spun to see who was watching him there was no one who stood out from the crowd.

He looked up to the upper rooms and roofs above. Nothing.

He peered down the alleys. Still nothing.

Maybe he was just getting paranoid.

Call us! Call us and we will make everything easier. Even Deathless Pirate was making promises now.

He tried to distract himself with conversation, leaning toward Etienne just as the other man took a scrap of paper surreptitiously from an outstretched hand of a man walking past. If he hadn't been watching at that exact second, he'd never have noticed the former Lord Mythos palming the scrap of white paper.

"Strange how all the cities of Jingen are laid out the same way, isn't it?" Tamerlan asked when Etienne looked sharply in his direction. Just a casual question. He hadn't seen anything. Or at least, that was what he was trying to project.

There was a flash of someone familiar up ahead near the canal. Just a flash of something in the thick rain. That wasn't Anglarok, was it? The Harbinger? It couldn't be. What would he be doing here?

Tamerlan felt a little chill run up his spine. Eyes. Watchers. Was he really doing the hunting, or was he hunted, too?

"It's not really that strange if you understand why," Etienne said, but he sounded distracted, too. Probably thinking about what was on the paper.

Every time Tamerlan saw him, Etienne was watching Tamerlan's hands shake and trying not to look too obviously at his eye. Tamerlan was no fool. Etienne didn't trust him. It didn't matter that they were allies in trying to track down the Grandfather. It didn't matter that he'd sealed their vow with magic. It didn't matter that they worked together every night in the refugee camps alleviating the worst of the misery – he still didn't trust Tamerlan.

He could never forget that Tamerlan had smoked the Spices just like he had and opened the Bridge of Legends just like he had. He could never forget that the evil that had possessed him and stolen Marielle was forged in the same flames as the good that possessed Tamerlan and gave his eye to bind the dragon again.

"It's a mandala," Etienne said.

"Like the ones the Timekeepers carry? And the patterns they walk it the prayer gardens behind their cathedrals?" Tamerlan asked.

He'd read about Timekeepers. He'd never been much taken by their religion – though the architecture was beautiful. He could sit all day just drawing the arches over their doors. But no. He didn't worship time. And now that he'd met Grandfather Timeless, he certainly never would.

"Precisely. Those are mandalas just like the streets and canals of the Five Cities."

"That's a very artistic way to design a city," Tamerlan said, smiling absently, like he was in his own daydream world. He didn't want Etienne to see that he was keeping an eye on his hand as they snaked between the long lines of people into an alley that skirted the back of the Timekeeper's Ivory Cathedral.

"It's not made that way for the art," Etienne said. "Tell me, Tamerlan, why do you think that we built our cities on the backs of the dragons?"

"So that you could slaughter innocent girls and be conveniently close to dump their blood all over the dragon's spines?" And this time the smile Tamerlan gave Etienne was cold and tight.

Etienne might not trust him, but Tamerlan didn't really trust Etienne either.

The other man gave him a sharp look.

"Watch that we haven't been followed," he snapped.

He was impressive. He was still talking casually as he unrolled his slip of paper, counting on Tamerlan to be looking the other way as he quickly read it. But Tamerlan hadn't been fooled. He read the paper over the shorter man's shoulder, even as the former Lord Mythos continued to speak.

"Blood is what binds the dragons in place, certainly, but we also spell them to remain docile and frozen. Otherwise, you'd still have dragons and as you've so elegantly put it, we'd still have to 'dump blood all over their spines' but they'd be able to move and flame and generally object to the whole process. This way, they lay still and sedated."

He paused and Tamerlan looked back over his shoulder. Was that a harpoon he glimpsed at the end of the alley? Maybe they really were being followed. A tingle ran down his spine.

He should have looked earlier, but if he had, he wouldn't have read the slip of paper.

"Does that mean that Jingen will rise again? I only bound him. There's no mandala on his back."

Etienne was still talking, though his tone had turned smug. He thought he'd tricked Tamerlan, didn't he?

"Likely he was stunned at first, but yes he will rise. That is what the streets are for. A mandala of power. And as things move along the mandala – in this case, feet and carts and boats – the magic is renewed and strengthened fresh every day. Now, pay attention, we are almost at the Cathedral."

Tamerlan turned around again and followed Etienne but he wasn't thinking about mandalas of power or city design. He wasn't even thinking about the glimpse of harpoon he'd seen. He was thinking about what he had read on that slip of paper.

Tonight. Dusk. If you are late, we will be gone.

-The Whisper.

Who was The Whisper and what games was Etienne playing while Tamerlan was trying to save the world?

5: Ivory Cathedral

Tamerlan

It would have looked like lurking to anyone watching, but as they stood, studying the Ivory Cathedral from the back alley, Tamerlan's mind was flooded with memories of the last time he'd stood in front of a cathedral. He rubbed his blind eye almost without thinking – a nervous tick he'd picked up. He'd never bothered with a patch. Other than being milky white, the eye looked fine.

He drew in a deep breath and tried not to remember what it had been like outside the Cathedral of the Clock, watching it burn to the ground as Marielle was trapped inside the clock right in front of it. He should have chosen differently. He should have chosen her.

"You're sure he's in there?" he whispered.

"According to my sources, but there's only one way to find out." Etienne led him further down the alley to the back side of the cathedral. "We climb."

Etienne looked down and Tamerlan hid his shaking hands behind his back. He could still climb. If there was a chance to get Grandfather Timeless – any chance at all – he would take it.

The failed leader is correct. I feel him close. Abelmeyer was not very complimentary where Etienne was concerned – none of the Legends were. They thought that any leader who lost their city couldn't be used for anything again.

Not true. I could think of a few uses for him.

Well, Lila had a different perspective, but in fairness, it would probably be worse to be useful to Lila than worthless to someone like Abelmeyer.

He's not as pretty as you are, but he's pretty enough for me.

And her comments always made him blush. Especially when he remembered she was looking at Etienne through his eyes – eye. With flaming cheeks, he grabbed Etienne's arm.

"We've chased him and lost him over and over. We need a better plan. A trap or some other way to hold him. Chasing him again and again with no plan is insanity."

"I have a plan," Etienne said shortly.

"Then explain it to me. Explain it, or I won't go in with you."

Etienne swallowed and for the first time he looked uncomfortable. "I've thought about this for a long time. You'll have to use the Eye of Abelmeyer. We'll grab him and when you get your hands on him, you'll use the Eye."

Tamerlan gasped. "It took one of my eyes last time."

"A terrible price," Etienne agreed, his face hard as a rock. "But I can think of no other option."

"Can't I just do that anywhere? I just decided to use it with the dragon and then he was bound. Why grab him at all if we plan to use the Eye. We could do that right here."

Etienne snorted. "Weren't you watching? The Eye only Binds. But if he jumps through space and time – and don't you think he might be doing that if he keeps eluding us? – then we would be binding him somewhere, but we wouldn't know where and someone else might find him a free him, nullifying your sacrifice. Besides, if we don't have him in hand, we can't put him back in the clock to free Marielle. So either you use the Eye like a fool and miss our chance, or we surprise him, then you use it and we can haul him off to the clock because we know where he is."

Tamerlan's mouth twisted sourly. This had been the plan all along. To steal his other eye. Fury bubbled up within him, but as quickly as it bubbled up, it dissolved again. Wouldn't he do anything to save Marielle?

"Lead on."

Etienne looked skeptical, but with a small shake of his head, he grabbed the masonry and began to climb.

Tamerlan looked around. Was anyone watching? It was broad daylight – but with the rain pelting down, it made sense that no one was looking up. Everyone on the street had been ducking low under hoods or canopies.

Smoke and I'll help you with the climb, Lila tempted him.

Smoke and I will bless your arm for battle, Abelmeyer offered.

Tamerlan cursed under his breath and hurried to climb after Etienne. The gaps between the stone were wide enough. He could do this part without help. Even with shaking hands.

You're a fool not to take our help. It's offered freely," Lila said.

If by 'free' she meant with all the strings possible tied to it, then sure, it was 'free.' He'd take it if he had to – but not unless it was either his life on the line or catching the Grandfather.

If you'd smoked that first night after you gave your Eye, we would have had him right away. You've wasted months for nothing. It's just blind pride and stubbornness that deprives you of the power you could have. Forget your arrogance. Come back to us. That was Deathless Pirate. His impatience was the most palpable.

"What makes you so good at this, Lord Mythos?" Tamerlan muttered as they climbed. The crack in the masonry he was holding was too narrow. He bit his lip and pushed harder.

There was a wide window just above them and Etienne angled toward it.

Watch it. You nearly lost your hold! Don't cling so tightly to the wall, it puts unnatural pressure on your muscles.

Easy for Lila to say. She wasn't the one trying to scale the side of a building in the rain with a sword tangling around her feet.

You could have smoked and then it would be me!

Ease up, Legend! I'm doing all I can, and I don't need a critique of every action in my head! He growled to himself, blowing rain from his eyelashes as he climbed.

Lean back! Hang from your fingertips instead of trying to pull your torso so tight to the wall!

He risked trying it her way and immediately the climb was easier.

See? I told you so!

If the opportunity presents itself, it will be I who take the boy to greatness. That was Abelmeyer.

Tamerlan scrambled over the ledge of the window into an empty room filled with dust and discarded items.

Etienne clenched his lips tightly together and gave Tamerlan a concerned look.

"Crazy yet?"

Tamerlan scoffed.

"You were muttering to yourself," Etienne said, still looking wary.

"Let's just find the Grandfather."

Had he been speaking to himself? Sometimes he didn't know anymore.

You were. This is all too much for you. Accept help!

"We had to come this way. They've doubled the guard on the doors. No outsiders. And you know as well as I do that if we don't surprise him, he'll slip away again. Just like he did last time. We grab him. You use the Eye. We finish this."

Etienne didn't need to explain it to him. Just because he was fighting voices in his head didn't mean he was a fool.

"Do you see me objecting?"

"Just don't go crazy before we get to him, okay?"

"Consider it my gift to you." What did you say to that? After all, he was pretty sure he was already crazy.

They moved across the floor of the abandoned room like ghosts. Tamerlan frowned at the tracks left in the dust, but if they didn't find what they were looking for before the tracks were discovered, then tracks would be the least of their worries.

How had Etienne learned to move so quietly? He was a mass of mysteries. A former ruler who could scale walls and sneak through buildings? There was more to his story than Tamerlan could guess. If he was smart, he would have abandoned the former ruler months ago – but how did you tell an ally to leave when he was the only one in the world who wanted the same thing you wanted? Even if that ally clearly hated you?

"The Grandfather is here," Etienne whispered confidently. "Hold your nerve and we'll get Marielle out of that clock."

Tamerlan nodded. Still allies. For now.

He'd been surprised when Etienne had vowed to save Marielle after they both fled H'yi. But he of all people knew that guilt was a powerful motivator.

The door opened without a squeak and they emerged onto a balcony that ran a ring around a huge room below – the main sanctuary of the cathedral. At one end a massive gear-powered clock ticked out the seconds. Rays of light shot dully through the stained glass, highlighting the clock but muted by the rain outside.

In the center of the sanctuary a round stage was set, surrounded by white-robed priests. Around the edge of the balcony, lamps were lit and a massive chandelier hung over the stage. And at the center of the stage, stood a figure in a top hat and cloak. The Grandfather.

Tamerlan's heart began to race. It was him! He really was there!

They had to get this right.

Could they be seen standing here behind the lights? He could only hope that those below were too focused on what they were doing to look up into the balcony.

Don't let him see you! One glance and he'll be gone!

Tamerlan didn't need Abelmeyer's warning. Last time he and Etienne had cornered the Grandfather in the middle of a crowded inn, he'd disappeared in the crowd before they could reach him. The time before that, it had been a crowded street and the Grandfather had turned a corner into an alley. They'd only been steps behind him, but when they entered the alley, he had vanished.

Focus! You need us now.

"Prepare to fight," Etienne whispered in Tamerlan's ear. "The priests will not give him up without a battle. And we need a hold on him before we use that Eye."

"We're going to kill priests?"

He felt shocked but Etienne's eye roll told him the other man had known this was coming all along.

Tamerlan's hands shook. And here was the choice. He could smoke and have the skill he needed to fight, or he could try to do this on his own. And either way he might have to kill people – people who had never harmed him and maybe never would. Could he even do that? Did he want to?

You have no training in the sword, Abelmeyer reminded him.

And you don't have the stomach to kill, Lila chimed in.

You need us. Deathless Pirate sounded gleeful. *How else will you use the Eye?*

Call us, Alchemist! Call us to your aid!

If nothing else, their eagerness should worry him, shouldn't it? But what other choice did he have? If he hesitated – or if he tried to fight on his own knowing full well that he didn't have the skills and might hesitate at the worst possible moment, then all would be lost – these two months of hunting and chasing and working with the man he hated – Etienne. All for nothing.

With shaking hands, he pulled the oilpaper package from his pocket and carefully extracted a single roll of Spices before returning it to safekeeping. He sidled up to a lamp and lit the end of the roll.

"Tsk." Etienne's sound conveyed all of his loathing and disapproval in one single sound.

"Do you want to win? Do you want me to use Abelmeyer's Eye? None of that happens without this." Tamerlan hissed.

He was doing the wrong thing.

The smoke smelled so good – it called to him like a familiar friend, replacing the scents of dust and old books with a haunting, enchanting smell. A smell that promised to take all his pain and guilt and indecision and hide it away for a while.

This had better work.

He tried not to think about what the cost would be. Blindness. Better not to think of that at all.

Below them, the voices of the priests drifted up.

"There are rumors that the Smudgers have gathered in the Hunsu District in a wide field. All of them. They work on a great spiritual work."

Who cared what the Smudgers were doing? They'd fled the cities like rats.

He put the roll to his lips and inhaled as much as he could. It surrounded him in puffs of grey and soft purple – an old friend, a fickle lover, a cruel king. The smoke that had haunted him for months was his now, filling his nose and mouth with quivering expectation.

Excitement and anticipation filled him, and he clenched his jaw in pain at the excitement reverberating across the bridge as the Legends battled to take over his body.

Die, Grandfather!

It never got easier. He shook with the passion of the Legend and the last threads of his own control, the Legend's anticipation mixing with his own expectation to create a feeling as addictive as ambition and as all-consuming as greed.

As the Legend seized his body and used it to climb up onto the railing of the balcony, it was hard not to try to clench his eye shut and scream. It's a horrible thing to give your future and the fate of your body into the hands of someone you can't possibly trust.

And it was also the most thrilling release – what happened next was going to be determined by someone else.

Trust me!

Byron Bronzebow! He hadn't expected that! Abelmeyer had felt the strongest. And he needed Abelmeyer to use the Eye.

I have tricks of my own. Next time, bring a bow. I'm sick of swords.

And then he was leaping from the railing, sailing out with a massive springing jump like an eagle leaping into flight. He sailed out over the sanctuary and caught the cable suspending the chandelier, swinging on it over the assembled priests and scattering hot dripping wax over all of them.

It was glorious. It was perfectly executed. Tamerlan's breath caught in his throat.

The Grandfather looked up.

Now! Use the Eye *now*!

Tamerlan dropped through the branches of the chandelier right on top of him.

His feet hit the ground with a smack. But where was the Grandfather? He should have felt the pain of smacking with full force onto the Legend's back or shoulder. Instead, nothing.

Byron whirled in Tamerlan's body, trying to see everywhere at once with one eye as he drew his sword, but there was nothing – no one there but stunned priests.

Their shocked expressions bloomed into snarls.

Tamerlan's heart kicked into high gear as they rushed toward him, drawing their own swords and knives in the whirl of their billowing robes. It was like a bush of roses had come to life to attack him, white petals whirling in the wind of anger.

Byron raised his blade, meeting the first lunge with a fast parry and spinning to the side between two priests. His pursuer couldn't get a clean swipe at him as the other two closed over his path. The white of their robes rolled in the breeze of their attack.

A fist swung toward him and he dodged the strike, ducking under it. He stabbed quickly, precisely, and a priest fell to the ground, red blossoming over his white robe.

Another spin and he cut down a second priest. A blow clipped the blind side of his head – hard enough to leave it ringing in pain but not hard enough to stop him. He whirled to the side and jabbed his sword in the belly of the man who had hit him.

"Get out of there!" Etienne called to him and he looked up from the fray in time to see him on the other side of the room near a small door.

Byron kicked out, striking one of the priests in the gut. As he hunched over in pain, Byron jumped up, stepping on the hunched man and leaping from his bent back to the shoulder of a shocked priest with a sword in each hand. Before the man could react, Byron was spinning into the air in a tucked tumble, sword still in hand.

He was going to skewer them like a lamb for Festival!

But his spinning roll brought them free of the priests, landing beside a cursing Etienne.

"You're a fool!" the other man spat as they ran through the door.

The guards on the other side turned in confusion at the same time that Byron grabbed the closest one by his collar and bashed his head against the wall. He didn't see what Etienne did to the other guard – that was his blind side. But he was still side by side with Tamerlan when they met the second pair at the main door.

Tamerlan spun in an arc of destruction, his sword whipping up so quickly that the guards could barely scream before blood spattered the wall and the ceiling and then they were running through the door of the cathedral and out into the downpour.

"He disappeared!" Etienne said between breaths as they ran out into the alley. "You dropped and he was gone before you landed!"

There hadn't been enough time to use the Eye. Which meant it had all been for nothing.

The smoking.

The killing.

The letting a Legend loose.

His hands were steady as a mountain. The shakes were gone as Byron piloted his body. But at what cost? His heart was sinking faster than a lead weight in the sea.

"Let's go do some good," he heard Byron say with his voice. What a load of trash. What good could possibly make up for all the evil done on this stormy day?

6: Queen Mer

Marielle

The smells were returning and with them, her sense of self was returning, too. Every burst of scent was effervescence to her – new life. Hope, perhaps.

She could almost scent her way as she tried to find her path through the tangles of history. The smell of the sea – aquamarine in its tangled scent and enticing in its salty embrace lapped against the Dragonblood Plains. The smell of the rivers and canals grass-green with growing life and thick with the scents of river plants and the fecundity of the rich soil lining the banks led her along. The musky smell of dragons sleeping deep under the rock – or wait now the smell of their musk was up in the air – was like a layer under everything else. A bedrock. The bones of the earth, the skeleton of history. She hadn't realized how tangled the dragons were with the lives of the people of the Dragonblood Plains until she smelled them under everything. And around everything else, flowing in and through and around was the scent of vanilla and lilac magic swirling in ribbons of turquoise and golden sparkles like a potent drug.

It was all the glorious smells that reminded her that she was Marielle. She was a Scenter. She was pledged to the Windfinders and pledged to justice.

She was not Time.

It was the smells that finally brought back her humanity. That reminded her of her loves and hates, of her attractions and petty irritations – of all the things that made her alive.

She blew through a crowd like the wind on the edge of a rocky seacoast. Alive, but a spirit here as she swam through time.

Ships bobbed in the distance. Around her, anticipation swirled in every whiff of breeze. The scent of cilantro filled the air and spring grass green swirls of color were everywhere. She studied faces. She watched flickers of fear in lightning blue puffs. Spurts of silver certainty. Hope in bronze rolling waves. They painted the crowd like the work of a master.

What time was she in? The clothing of the people was different – older, like her grandfather's grandfather's clothing. But the people were the same – the same expressions, the same scents swirling in them, the same feeling of a crowd that was looking to a central figure.

The figure rose up on steps to a makeshift platform and Marielle startled when she realized what she was seeing. That wasn't …?

It couldn't be.

But the scent was all right – exactly as she would have guessed it would be. Power, smelling like gardenias and rolling from this figure in ribbons of royal blue mixed with a residual scent of the turquoise salt of the sea.

She was tall – that was to be expected. And harsh – of course. She had a nose she could have stolen from a hawk – that Marielle wouldn't have guessed. History had forgotten the nose. But far from her statues, which were always swathed in white and shells, she wore only a simple fisherwoman's dress. And her hair – far from the flowing locks tangled with starfish and seashells – was cropped around her shoulders in a no-nonsense cut that kept it out of her way.

But glory swirled around her in byzantine purple, swallowing up the blue and turquoise as if this moment was so significant that it dwarfed everything else. It tinged the platform and the crowd and even spread into the distance until all Marielle could see was purple.

The woman began to speak and the crowd fell silent.

"From the sea lies our only hope. A people set apart unaffected by what we do here today. You saw me send the families forth. They will be protected from our choices here."

What was she talking about? Was she talking about the renowned time in history when Queen Mer sent her people out, telling them to never rest or stop until they found the story that would make sense of everything?

Marielle felt a thrill run up her spine. She was watching history. She was seeing it with her own eyes! But in the history books,

Queen Mer hadn't been a plain fisherwoman with a hawk nose. She'd been a beautiful and glorious queen who sang to the sea and stopped it from raging, who sang to the land and ended the civil wars.

"You judge me for what I did. You say I banished them. You say I sent them to die. But you know just as I do, that we have no other choice. Someone must be saved to live on. And someone must stay to fight. Together – and only together – we can end this constant cycle of civil wars. If we don't – none of us will be left to feel resentment."

Someone beside Marielle snarled and she looked at his face – at the garnet rage that rolled off him filling her nose with the scent of pitch.

"There'd be no war without the dragons!" He cried. "No war if they didn't steal our children!"

The woman with the hawk nose spun to look at him, pointing through the crowd.

"I am one of you! I saw my sister dragged through the streets and hung upside down as they opened her throat to feed the dragon! I fought beside you in the first uprising. And the second. We tore down the Lords. We raised our own. And what did it get us?"

"Choan writhes beneath us!" someone called.

"Yes," the woman said. "The dragon stirs. Our fate hangs in the balance, yet still, we fight, neighbor fighting neighbor. Homes and livelihoods stolen in the night. But today we change that."

She pulled something from a sack she was holding – a sack Marielle hadn't even noticed that she had.

"I took this crown from Lord Y'ni." The woman lifted the crown up high. Even from here, Marielle could smell the faint traces of blood and violence drifting off the crown. "I cut it from his head while he still lived. I claim it now."

She jammed the crown on her head, glaring at the crowd as if she dared them to say anything about what she was doing. A chunk of something that looked like dried fur was stuck to one of the points of the crown.

"I am your queen now. Queen Mer of the Sea. And I will end the fighting in the streets and unite you all beneath the tide I bring with me."

Behind her there was a roar, as tentacles reached up out of the sea, framing the hawk-nosed woman like a crown of the sea. Marielle gasped. The Kratoen! She'd heard rumors of the mighty Kratoen, the creature of the sea enchanted by Queen Mer to do her bidding, but like all other stories, she'd thought it was only a legend. Yet here he was.

The tentacles curled and snatched at floating wreckage – wreckage that Marielle hadn't noticed until now. It wasn't the only one. Had there been a sea battle out on the raging waves? How many ships had sunk to leave that many wrecks behind? And had Queen Mer been the cause of that?

Marielle looked around her. There were no children in the crowd. The people were coated in mud and blood. They carried makeshift weapons. Had there just been a battle here?

In the heady feeling of finally scenting again – and of seeing a living moment of history – she hadn't even noticed the residue of war all around her.

The tentacles disappeared back into the sea with a crash and the spray of the water they smacked as they left misted the crowd.

"I baptize you with my reign. I claim you as my people!"

"What about our daughters and sons? What about their blood?" someone in the crowd yelled. Perhaps that was what they had been fighting about.

"No more will we steal your children," Queen Mer called out and the roar of the crowd swept up so strongly that the ground beneath Marielle seemed to tremble with it.

"Then how will we bind the dragon?" someone else called when the roar died down.

"From here on, we will purchase any person we take from willing families. Yes, we need the blood of the dragonblooded to keep us safe, but no more will you fear the kidnapping or quelling of your overlords. We will only take the willing – those willing to give themselves."

But those around Marielle asked the question she wished she could still ask. "Who would be willing?"

But the answer was there a moment later – there in her memory. Who would do it? Anyone who needed a second chance that money could provide.

She tasted bitterness on her tongue at the thought. Lord Mythos claimed that her own mother had been willing to give Marielle's life to the dragon. And before that, Tamerlan's father had been willing to give his sister. There was no telling what a person would give for the right price. When wealth greased the wheels to your dreams, no price was too steep for hope.

"Not only for this," Queen Mer said, "but for everything. We will not take your sons and daughters without recompense."

The crowd cheered, but Marielle's heart sank. She'd just watched Queen Mer sell the souls of her people's children for generations to come.

Queen Mer was supposed to be the savior of the five cities of the Dragonblood plains – the mother of the People of Queen Mer who lived only on the sea. She'd stopped the endless cycle of internal wars – hadn't she?

What Marielle had just seen didn't quite line up with what she'd been told.

But she had watched it. She was no longer inhuman floating in time. She could see things now. She could learn. And maybe, just maybe, she could find her way out of the trap the Grandfather had put her in.

7: Stalking Shadows

Tamerlan

It didn't feel right to have someone else running his body even when they were doing something good. And the looks Etienne kept shooting at him told Tamerlan that he knew exactly what was going on here. But he couldn't be more condemning of Tamerlan than Tamerlan was of himself. He knew exactly how guilt-soaked he was. He was sodden to the core.

And that made him just a bit angry. Because what was he supposed to have done? What would anyone else have done? Not everyone could be Etienne who could apparently do anything. Tamerlan hadn't even seen him descend to the lower level or get past the priests. And who knew how he learned to climb like that!

They'd fled the temple, cleaned up in the canal, and then Byron had sped along the canal to the Trade District, broken into a warehouse, and stolen a barge and filled it with grain. Tamerlan hadn't been surprised when he sped down the river toward the refugee camp.

Neither had Etienne.

"This will wear off soon, and then you'll be wanted by the authorities," he said dryly as they drew near to the camp. "And then you'll have to hide from more than just the shadows that you are sure are stalking you in the night."

Byron ignored him. He was a man on a mission – as always.

"I know that you're in there, Tamerlan," Etienne pressed. "Take control of yourself and stop this before it's too late."

As if killing a bunch of priests hadn't already been bad enough. As if he'd had any other choice. What was he supposed to do? How else was he supposed to capture the Grandfather? It was just too hard to fight with your hands tied behind your back!

"Take courage, good man. Justice will prevail," Byron said with his lips.

"Uh-huh. And so will the guards when this Legend is done with you. Once this grain is distributed there will be no more hiding. Everyone will have seen your face."

"Do not speak to me of flouting the authorities," Byron said. "We saw your note. You foment revolution."

Etienne's expression turned stony. "That's not your affair."

"Revolution is a dangerous thing," Byron lectured him. "Better to help the people from behind the scenes and let them decide when to make a move. If you force their hands there may not be the result you wish. I saw a man force a revolution once – he only ended with his head on a pole and it was put there by the people he was trying to help! Better to shame the rulers until the people see for themselves."

"You're shaming something, alright," Etienne muttered.

And his resentment was understandable, but Tamerlan wasn't the only one with secrets in his heart. And it was hard to feel much compassion for Etienne now. After all, it was Etienne's plan to take the rest of his vision. One eye hadn't been enough.

The barge hit the bank, sliding up beside a make-shift dock. And as always when he came here, Tamerlan's heart lurched.

A group of children ran toward the dock, their elders hanging back not certain what to think of a strange barge. All of them were dressed in worn, dirty clothing and soaked to the bone in the rain. The shelters here were abysmal. Firewood hard to find. If it were this bad in autumn, how much worse would it be in winter?

And it was winter that Tamerlan feared for these people – for the people he had betrayed and damned to this refugee camp.

It was hard not to agree with Bronzebow. What could it hurt to help these people? Even if it meant stealing, wasn't that a small crime compared to the ones he'd already committed?

See? I will make you a proper thorn in these Landholds' flesh in no time!

And he wanted that. If it wasn't for Marielle in the clock, he would stay here with Byron forever righting this great wrong – and they would build an orphanage.

I was raised in an orphanage. I could devote myself to that, yes.

Bronzebow leapt from the prow and hurriedly tied up the barge, lifting up a small child of about five.

"And what is your name, little dragon?"

The child laughed, "Is that food on that boat?"

"It is!" he said with a laugh and the warmth flooding Tamerlan was partly his own and partly Bronzebow's. "Go get your parents!"

Squeals filled the air as the children ran into the rain and it was only moments later that their tired-eyed elders arrived, drenched and uncertain. It was as if they were afraid to hope. As if hope would sear worse than the scars already lacing their souls.

"Help me get this grain out of the rain!" was all Bronzebow had to say with Tamerlan's voice, and then they were there, pressing in with silent desperation.

He moved grain for almost an hour, handing sacks in the pouring rain to one desperate almost-hoping face after another. The worn hands of mothers clung to him with thanks on their lips and tears in their eyes. Fathers with new lines etched into their faces threw sacks up onto their shoulders, gathering a child or two up with them as they hurried away. The grain wouldn't be enough. Not for the whole winter. But it might get them that far, at least.

It was enough for now. For this moment.

Etienne worked beside him until the barge was empty and the two of them were left exhausted in the hull.

"I don't like seeing my people like this," Etienne said. "The rulers of Yan make them dependent on that dole. It breaks their spirits. Doles rob a man of his independence, of his self-respect, of his calling."

"Maybe not for long," one of the refugees said, leaning in close in the rain. He was a dark-haired man with a limp. He clung to his bag of grain like he was afraid someone might snatch it away. "If you want hope, look for the tent of Variena. She has plans for us."

Clearly, he thought they were refugees, too.

"Variena?" Etienne asked and his tone was cool. Tamerlan had noticed his tone tended to grow cool when he was considering deeper things than what was on the surface. "The Red Door Woman from Jingen?"

"You've heard of her, then." The man sounded satisfied. "Follow me."

Etienne stood up quickly and Bronzebow followed. What made him interested in this woman? Tamerlan had never heard of her and they'd been working to help the people in these camps for weeks.

But never like this. This gift has brought the attention of the true power in this refugee camp. We should meet them. We can help them.

In truth, he hadn't really hurt anything, had he? After all, while stealing grain was wrong, distributing it to the needy made up for that, right?

I agree. Let's meet this Variena and see how we can help her.

They slid through the descending darkness of the camp, skidding in the thick mud churned up by many feet and relentless rain. Shelters here hardly counted as shelters at all. Some were nothing more than blankets or rugs strung up between poles. Smoke wisped up from some of the better shelters – muted and faint as the fires struggled to stay lit.

Etienne had called them his people, but in truth there were are many here from H'yi as there were from Jingen.

It was to one of the shelters with a fire that the man led them. Ringed with people even in the rain, the shelter was a simple place. Carpets – their colorful designs mud-streaked now – and an actual tarpaulin formed a crude pavilion packed with bodies. From the edges, it was hard to see the struggling fire but there was a heat in the eyes of the people crowded here. They were mostly men – young men – and they all seemed moments away from violence. Growls of agreement rippled through their ranks as words were muttered between them.

At the center, a woman was talking, her face lit with emotion.

Tamerlan's heart seized, his breath coming too quickly.

Was that?

It couldn't be.

Marielle!

But it wasn't. The woman turned and her eyes met his. Brown eyes – not Marielle's purple ones. And the lines on her face showed a woman almost twenty years older than Marielle. But still, his breath caught in his throat.

"Her mother," Etienne whispered in his ear right before he grabbed Tamerlan's arm and dragged him into the shadows. "Shhh. Say nothing. We can't be here right now. I have somewhere I need to be, and you need to get back to Jhinn. Now."

And stop mooning over women twice your age.

That was Lila's voice. Somewhere in that moment when he'd seen Variena, Byron Bronzebow had left him.

Tamerlan blinked. She'd looked so much like Marielle. It felt like a punch to the gut to see her. He wanted to talk to her. He wanted to see if she was like Marielle.

"Tamerlan." He looked up to see Etienne's eyes boring into his in the half-light. "I know what you're thinking. Don't talk to her. She's more dangerous than you realize. Go and find Jhinn. We need a plan to find the Grandfather again. Maybe this time, you'll be quicker in using that Eye."

Tamerlan flinched as he nodded. He'd been too slow. Had it been because he hesitated to lose his vision? By the time they tried again, he'd need to be over that fear just in case.

After a moment, Etienne patted him on the shoulder with a satisfied nod before slipping away into the shadows. The darkness and rain swallowed him up before he'd gone more than a few steps.

Tamerlan breathed in a long breath. He should listen to Etienne and go back to Jhinn. The other man would be waiting. It made sense. And yet …

He couldn't stop thinking about Variena. She'd looked so much like her daughter. And everyone was hanging on her words. Perhaps he could listen just for a few moments. He crept through the shadows toward the edge of the crowd, listening, watching.

There she was! Her eyes glowed in the light of the fire and the favor of the crowd.

"You saw how the Landholds treated us! They bought my daughter's life to save our city. My daughter! And the city was still destroyed by the dragon. What was the point of her sacrifice? What was the point of any of the sacrifices? We've been tricked! We've all been made fools of by those with money and power. They tread on our heads as their walkways. They make our broken bodies their roads. It's all been a lie!"

She didn't know. Her daughter was alive, and she didn't know!

Tamerlan took a step forward.

Pain split through his head, stopping him mid-stride and the world went dark.

8: Searching through Time

MARIELLE

It was as hard to steer herself through the tides of history as it was to steer a maple seed through the course of a river – and yet, she was making progress.

And now she'd stumbled on two Legends together.

It was Maid Chaos – or she thought it was. Her hair was long and gleaming, and her curving figure seemed better suited to dancing than sitting in a dark room drinking with a one-eyed man.

"I didn't fight this hard to gain power just to see it slip away," she said and the bitterness in her words seemed far too deep for one so young. "They're my people – my followers. Mine. Do you hear me?"

She smelled – wrong. Like a dog with rabies. An astringent scent close to Elderflower. And her colors were too bright – like they'd been infected with something. Marielle had seen that before and she knew exactly what it was. In the City Watch, you found people like this sometimes. Occasionally, they were harmless. More often, their crimes turned your stomach worse than rotted meat ever could. Insanity was not a pleasant scent even if the scent itself was not so bad.

"If the dragons stay free, you'll lose any power you have. They're picking us off village by village. They are too large – too powerful." That was King Abelmeyer – she was sure of it. From his single eye to the ruby hanging in the frame of his open-laced shirt, he was all king. Scent trails of Royal blue wrapped around him like a cloak – a testament to his power.

"The price is too high. The people will revolt," she said, her insanity flaring so that a burst of rainbow colors spun around her. "You've planned this to quell us all, haven't you? Planned it to make yourself King of all the Dragonblood Plains!"

He sighed. "I don't care about crowns. They're too heavy for an honest head. And I don't care about power. It's nothing but an anvil pulling me deeper and deeper into hell. I just want to save who I can. While I can."

"Then do it by yourself."

He opened his palms, showing them to her – empty. "I can't. I'm just not enough."

"You stopped that dragon when you gave your eye."

"But only temporarily. To keep him bound will require more. And I don't have more to give."

What did that mean for Tamerlan and his sacrifice outside the clock? She'd seen him give an eye – hadn't she? Or was that King Abelmeyer? Had she seen that with her own eyes or had she watched Abelmeyer in the flows of history? Sometimes it was hard to keep the two straight. She'd seen too much of what had been and what would be and what might have been. Marielle's mind felt fuzzy and thick.

"You have another eye," Maid Chaos said glibly, but it was lightning blue fear that tinged her words, not levity.

Abelmeyer's growl made Marielle feel her own thrill of fear even though he couldn't see her. His voice was hard as flint.

"You'll do this, you trumped-up maid. And you'll do it when I tell you, or I'll shake you to pieces. Like a dog with a rat in its mouth."

The scene started to fade. Marielle tried to claw her way back. What happened next? Did Maid Chaos agree to work with Abelmeyer or did he manage to force her? Why did the histories never talk of this? Marielle was dying to know.

What had he needed from her to seal the dragon up and why was Maid Chaos so nervous about the cost?

But the scene faded, and Marielle was rolling again in the river of time, bobbing just along the surface. She had found no laws to this place – no code. There was nothing to govern what she – or anyone – should or shouldn't do and that terrified her to the core. She was a servant of justice, not a filmy seed in the wind.

But justice worked best when the judge knew all the facts. And there was more to find in this morass of history – if she could just steer herself to the right things.

Grimacing mentally, she pushed on.

9: Kidnapped

Tamerlan

"He's waking now."

The voice sounded familiar, but Tamerlan's head was pounding so painfully that he might not have been able to pick out his own sister's voice in the heavy drumming going on inside his skull.

Pull yourself together. You have been captured. This is a time to keep your wits about you.

Deathless Pirate rarely gave advice. Strange that he was speaking to Tamerlan now.

The story is getting more interesting. I want to know who these people are who have our vessel in their hands.

Tamerlan blinked, opening crusty eyes. He was tied tightly to a chair. His hands and wrists hurt from the ropes and his back ached from where he'd been slumped in the hard chair. He was still soaking wet, though the room was dry, and a fire burned in the hearth. That meant he couldn't have been there for long.

He frowned. It looked like the room of an inn. Who would bring a kidnapped victim here? Anyone could hear his screams.

A face loomed into his vision. Ah. He recognized this one. The friend of Marielle. What was his name again? Anglarok.

"Remember me?" Anglarok asked with a smile that wasn't friendly at all.

"Sure," Tamerlan allowed. His lips felt thick and his mouth was dry.

"Remember this?" The man bounced the yellow conch shell on his palm – the same one Tamerlan had picked up when he found it in front of the clock. It was Marielle's.

"Yes."

"It's not yours," the other man said.

"Not yours either," Tamerlan replied. A drink would be nice right now.

Stop being so surly. Try to charm them!

Maybe that was easy for a pirate. It was hard for an Alchemist's apprentice. Especially when the people they were referring to had kidnapped him.

Stop fussing about how hurt you are by their actions – that's what children do. Adults deal with things as they are. Try to learn why they want you. That will give us valuable information.

"We want the girl that you put in the clock. We saw her there," Anglarok said. "Found her after many days of searching.

Alone. Alive in an undamaged clock, while the city around her was nothing but a burned husk. It took us weeks to find witnesses but did you really think we would stop. Did you really think we wouldn't look everywhere?"

"Why do you want Marielle?" Tamerlan asked. It seemed ridiculous to answer the rest. He hadn't thought about these people at all. Why would he?

There was the woman behind him – she had short cropped hair except for a long swath at the very front and she wore a furious expression that made him think of a Watch Officer, though she was clearly a foreigner. That must be the woman who Marielle had saved. Liandari. Was that right? He wasn't sure.

"She is ours. She took the vow. She is part of the Harbingers now and we owe her a debt. And the witnesses told us that a man with short blond hair put here there. A tall man. Broad-shouldered and confident, but with a beardless young face. He had a ruby medallion." Anglarok pulled the medallion around Tamerlan's neck out from under his shirt, twisting it until Tamerlan gagged. "This looks like a medallion to me. What do you think, Liandari?"

"If that's not a ruby medallion, then I'm an octopus," Liandari said. She slid a knife from its sheath and began to sharpen it slowly.

"We want her back," Anglarok said slowly.

He eased up on the chain and Tamerlan sucked in a gasping breath.

"I want her out of the clock as badly as you do." His words were rasping through his ragged throat.

It seemed the safest thing to say. This man looked violent and the gleam in his eye spelled trouble in capital letters.

Make him believe it!

"I'd do anything to get her out. But to do that, I have to find the Grandfather – the man who put her in the clock. And I need to trap him."

The blow came out of nowhere. Tamerlan's face blossomed with pain and the sight in his single eye went dark for a moment before he was spitting blood and gasping for breath.

These were Marielle's friends? These thugs?

"Don't lie to us," Liandari said from behind Anglarok. She stood at the fire, still sharpening her knife and swirling her fingers through his things. A few loose coins. A belt knife. A tangle of string. Abelmeyer's Eye. The rolls of Spices. Tamerlan flinched at the sight of those in her possession. What would she do with those? Did she know what they were?

"I'm not lying," Tamerlan said through a fat lip.

The blow came so fast that he couldn't flinch before it struck him, spinning his head with the force of it.

"Anglarok could hit you all day. But what would be the point of that? Better to be honest," Liandari said. He was starting to worry about that knife. What was she sharpening it *for?* "You put the girl in the clock. We can't get her out. You took her conch shell. And yet, you have not used it. But Anglarok smells the same scent on you that we smelled when the Lord Mythos vanished after promising to help us. The same smell that led us to the clock and Marielle. What is that smell, boy?"

Tamerlan kept his mouth shut now. He was learning his lesson.

Liandari picked up the contents of his pockets, examining them in her hands and he held his breath as she looked at the spices held in her hands.

In his mind, the Legends held their breath, too, because what he feared was the same thing that they wanted. They wanted her to burn the spices – whether for herself or for him. They wanted her to release them. He could almost feel them jockeying for position on the edge of the Bridge.

"I will give you a few minutes to think about how easy it will be for us to kill you and how wise it would be for you to tell us everything. In the meantime, Anglarok and I will have a quiet talk with the keeper of this fine inn. Rest assured that when we are done, any sound you make in the questioning will not concern him."

She threw his sword and the yellow conch shell on the table but the other things she kept in her hand as Anglarok opened the door to the room. Tamerlan heard the hinges squeaking behind him.

"Remember, boy," Liandari said. "Cities aren't the only thing that can be burned to the ground."

She threw his other things into the fire, as if for emphasis, or maybe to remind him that she could burn him just as easily –

and then the two of them stalked out of the room and shut the door.

Tamerlan waited for them to leave before sucking in as deep of a breath as he could.

Please let there be smoke! Please!

There! Just a whiff. Would it be enough?

He coughed. Breathed in more. Coughed again.

He was going to hyperventilate like this!

And then he wasn't coughing at all.

Ram the Hunter was coughing.

Yes! If anyone could get free, it was Ram!

Dragon. I sense it beneath us.

And then Ram the Hunter was bursting out of the bonds. How had he done that when he only had Tamerlan's muscles to use? And Ram the Hunter was scooping up Tamerlan's sword and strapping it on.

We hunt!

Ram reached to where Abelemeyer's Eye had landed – just the ruby part in the fire – and snatched it out, gripping it by the cooler chain.

Ram grabbed the chair he'd been tied to only moments before and ran to the window, shattering the panes with the chair legs and sweeping them clear before leaping up to the ledge.

The door to the room swung open and Anglarok charged in.

"What -?" shock was on his face, but it only took him a moment to snatch up his harpoon from beside the door.

"Next time," Ram growled. "Ask better questions."

And then he leapt out the window, grabbing a sign on the way down and swinging dramatically on it before landing squarely on the cobbles. Liandari rushed out the inn door, sword in hand. Anglarok was already up on the window ledge. How were they moving so fast? How had Liandari even known to run out the door? They were smarter than Tamerlan was. Quicker than he was.

Not quicker than Ram.

The sign over the door read, *The Priest's Revenge.* They were on the edge of the Temple District where trade and mercantile leaked into the edges of religion. That was a relief. He wouldn't have to go far for aid.

Fortunately, Ram was not hesitant. He was moving before Tamerlan had even assessed the situation, dashing down the cobbled street and between clumps of strangers working in the dusk of the first night of Autumngale – the night known as "Drawing Bounds." Tonight, groups of friends, family and neighbors would draw thick boundaries in chalk – or even oil pastels to defy the rain – all through the cities of the Dragonblood Plains. The boundaries marked the small places claimed by these groups of allies.

In the past, we didn't do it with chalk. We did it with blood.

Yuck. Of course, it would be something violent and unnecessary.

Who are you to say it wasn't necessary?

They ran through the rain, picking up speed as they dashed down to the canal. Ram tossed the Eye's chain over his head as he ran. Tamerlan could just imagine Ram out with a bucket of blood and paintbrush making marks on the streets.

That's too literal. What I mean is, we killed for what is ours. And I sense a dragon sleeping beneath our feet. We should slay this beast.

Did you ever slay dragons in your past life, Ram? Ram? Ram?

The Legend was gone.

Dragon's blood in a cup!

Feet pounded behind him and Tamerlan clenched his teeth. Just when he needed him the Legend was gone! It was up to Tamerlan to get free on his own, now. But what Ram could do with Tamerlan's body, Tamerlan could do … right?

He dashed toward the bridge, dodging knots of people with open mouths and wide eyes. They could gape all they wanted. He wouldn't get this chance twice.

Three more strides took him to the Echo Bridge and then he was jumping up onto the slick rock-work rails and leaping into the canal below.

Hopefully, Jhinn was where he'd left him.

Hopefully, he was faster and smarter than the Harbingers were.

Hopefully, he knew a good way to dry out on a rainy night.

He was almost laughing as he dropped through the air.

10: VISIONS OF A FUTURE PAST

MARIELLE

She was getting closer to where she wanted to be. Floating. Drifting from moment to moment, life to life. One moment she was watching as a child helped her father stack rocks to build their neighborhood wall – drawing bounds to keep enemies out. They were full of hope and delight – bronze and apple red swirling around them in a way that made her want to sing with shared delight. A moment later she was watching that same woman – old now and bent – fighting on her small neighborhood wall. She cut back attackers with a knife the length of her forearm. Maybe she won. Maybe she died there defending her home. Marielle didn't see, though a part of her knew. A part of her knew everything.

And yet, when you know everything, but you're still human, it's impossible to know it all at once. Impossible, that is, if you want to keep your humanity. Impossible, if you want to keep your sanity.

So, Marielle let herself drift. She let herself cry tears of devastation as she watched one life after another burst forth, live, and then crumple and fade and die. Knowing everything was more painful than she'd ever imagined. And more beautiful.

And then her nose caught a familiar smell and just like that, she didn't want to know anything at all except for this. It was just like the first time she'd scented it – when she'd known somehow that life would never be the same again.

She didn't know how she followed it, but she did, squeezing between lives and memories, pushing past epic stands and bold speeches, ducking under the tables where back-door dealings were made. The golden scent twisted in the air around her, drawing her closer, closer, closer.

And then she was standing in a field and she was watching a boy with huge bright eyes staring at the sky. He was drawing birds in flight with a charcoal on a small scrap of paper and his faraway smile spoke of an imagination alive with the delight of living. Behind him, a little girl with long hair and chubby hands, stalked up through the grass, trying to look up at what he was seeing.

"They're only starlings," she said.

But his smile grew.

And gold surrounded him.

And then the scene slipped away.

Marielle clawed desperately for it, trying to go back, trying to find it again.

She found him briefly – a little younger this time – running as fast as he could, trying to catch a rainbow in a field that seemed just out of reach, his little face screwed up with concentration and absolute infatuation rolling off him in pink waves. And then he was gone again, as insubstantial as the rainbow had been.

She would find him again. The golden scent still drew her. It still curled through the air before her. He was out there somewhere. And she would find him.

Tamerlan.

11: HUNTING TIME

TAMERLAN

It had all been a terrible disaster. Tamerlan's hands shook as they slid up the canal in the Government District through the damp darkness. Though for once they weren't shaking from wanting to smoke – just from nerves and excitement. The moon hung in the sky like a single eye – mocking Tamerlan for losing his.

"I don't know why you feel bad about smoking, boy," Jhinn scolded quietly from his seat in the stern of the gondola. "It gives you the power to change destinies. Sometimes for the bad, sure, but lots of times for the good."

He seemed unruffled by Tamerlan's sudden drop into the gondola. He hadn't even batted an eye when Tamerlan had demanded that they flee the area.

Tamerlan snorted. "Name one time it was for the good."

Jhinn's long dry pause was only interrupted by his drier tone. "That time you brought a dragon down from the sky."

"How about the time I woke one up?" He couldn't help the bitterness of his tone. "Or the time I killed a lot of priests for no reason."

"You said they were harboring the Grandfather."

"Yes."

"You know they worship him, right? They worship a horrific Legend that will feast on their bones someday." Jhinn's grin made it hard to tell whether he felt that was awful or funny.

"Yes." Tamerlan was answering, but his eyes scanned the silhouettes of the buildings they passed. Was anyone watching them?

"And when you were done killing people who are already dead, what happened?" Jhinn demanded.

Tamerlan shivered. At least it was quiet and sleepy here. No one would hear Jhinn naming his crimes so loudly.

"I don't know why you insist on thinking that anything on the land is dead, Jhinn." Better to change the subject. "You know that I leave and come back to you and when I'm on your gondola I'm alive."

"And what is your point, boy?" The younger boy leaned into the turn as they slid through into narrower channel. "The dead act in strange ways. And some of them come back to haunt me."

Tamerlan couldn't help but smile under the cloak of darkness – a whimsical smile. Imagine living a life where everything outside the boats didn't exist to you? Imagine living with the same few people on the water day after day, year after year, trading with those you think of as ghosts for food and supplies. He could imagine it. It felt – beautifully foreign. Like a song in a different language.

When he'd freed Marielle and started his orphanage and no one was left empty and fatherless and alone, then he was going to go and explore the world. He was going to see all the places and meet all the people and write down their beautiful tragedies and peculiarly attractive notions in a book. And he would call it the Book of Hearts and it would be in a Library where everyone could read it and …

"You dreaming again, boy? What happened after you killed all those priests?"

Tamerlan sighed. He wouldn't be writing a book today. "We stole a boat and fed the refugees."

"You brought food to the poor on a boat?" Jhinn snorted. "Yes, I can see why you're worried. Terrible deeds done tonight. They will fear your name in the canal gossip and set charms to keep you at bay."

"Laugh all you want. It's dangerous to call the Legends. And I did it twice. Once to get the Grandfather. Once to fight those Harbingers."

Jhinn spat. "That was wise. You must avoid the Retribution at all costs. Accept nothing from them!"

Tamerlan felt his jaw gingerly. Jhinn had helped him find dry clothes after his own were soaked in the canal – why were they always guard's clothes? Did Jhinn have a secret connection with the Palace Guard pursers? – and he'd helped apply a salve to Tamerlan's injuries, but they still stung.

"All I got from them was a beating."

"Be sure it stays that way. They are dangerous people."

Tamerlan pulled the yellow shell from his belt pouch. It was wet but intact. He looked at in the light of the moon. They'd said they'd given it to Marielle. Had it been dangerous to her? The opening of the Bridge of Legends by Etienne had been what sealed her fate. Not this shell.

Jhinn's breath drew in sharply. "They gave you that?"

"It was Marielle's. They say they gave it to her."

"Don't touch it. It's cursed."

"How?"

"Just don't touch it, okay? Put it away. And then pay attention. We need to sneak now. We're almost there."

Tamerlan tucked the shell away and looked up. Jhinn was right. They were almost to the tall building at the University District. The one Lila kept harping on.

I told you. Get us to that building. Open the Bridge, and I'll take care of everything.

But that was what he was worried about.

I won't kill anyone. This time. We'll just break into the palace and find the Library. You and Etienne couldn't get into it without discovery. The Palace library will have what we need – books you haven't read yet about the Grandfather. The key will be in there somewhere and then we can find him again. Or do you want to spend another two months searching every hidey hole from here to the sea?

Besides, there might be a suggestion in one of those books for a solution that doesn't leave you blind.

He didn't even have months. Not with Marielle stuck in that clock. How long would she keep her humanity? How long would it be until she lost herself entirely?

He gritted his teeth.

"Can you hear them talk to me, Jhinn?" he whispered. "The Legends? They never stop."

"I've noticed," Jhinn said, but his eyes were on their goal. "But you could probably quiet them if you wanted to."

He couldn't. He'd tried and he couldn't.

"Anyone else would think I was mad."

"Mad is better than blind," Jhinn said, still distracted. "That Lord Mythos doesn't even see them."

But was it better? He could never escape their cloying words, dragging him deeper and deeper into their view of the world.

You already smoked the Spice twice tonight, Lila crooned. *Just do it one more time. Just do it with me.*

She could be so charming when she was trying. And it was so easy to listen. Especially right now when he'd just smoked twice before. After all, if he'd already compromised his morals, what was one more time? He could stop again tomorrow and never do it again.

Exactly.

It couldn't hurt for this. And there was no other way he was going to get into the palace. Etienne said it wasn't worth the risk. There were guards posted at every gate. And they were alert in these troubled times. He'd already waited for hours on other nights, staring at this palace and wondering how to get in.

And it will feel good.

This was the only way.

"What did she mean about you going blind?" Jhinn asked. "Is your good eye troubling you?"

"Etienne wants me to trap the Grandfather by sacrificing my other Eye," Tamerlan said, surprised by the calmness in his voice. He didn't feel that calm.

Jhinn snorted.

"Tell Etienne that he has two eyes. He can sacrifice one before he makes you lose the other. There is more than one way to fillet a catfish."

Tamerlan's fingers drifted up to touch the ruby necklace under his shirt. "I don't think I'd trust Etienne to do that. He has his own purposes."

Jhinn eased the gondola into a shadowy mooring. "Then I guess you should go to the land of the dead and get us some information. Find another way. I'll wait here for you."

Tamerlan leapt from the gondola with the coil of rope they'd brought with them. "If I don't come back in an hour, get out of here. I don't want you to get caught up in this."

Jhinn rolled his eye. "Are the dead speaking to me again? It must only be my imagination."

It was such a silly belief. But sometimes Tamerlan wished it was true. He wished it was true as he stalked into the shadows at the base of the looming Court of Trespasses. After all, if it were true, he would be guiltless. He'd never committed any crimes on the water.

And if it were true, then he wouldn't be the only fool listening to people who weren't even there.

He wished it was true as he pulled out a roll of spice and lit it in the street brazier. Wished it was true as he wet his lips with his tongue and then brought the roll up to it, sucking in the sweet, sweet smoke of power.

And the Bridge opened.

And Lila Cherrylocks grabbed his body so fast and hard that he stumbled.

Sorry, pretty man. I didn't want to risk anyone else grabbing harder than me this time. Let's go find the Grandfather.

She drew a breath of smoke through the roll of paper and another and another. Why was she being so amenable? He thought he'd have to negotiate with her.

She threw the paper aside and stepped on it and then she was scaling the slick stone walls of the Court building, climbing with a speed he'd never possessed.

I like breaking into places. Besides, it occurs to me that if I do what you want from time to time, you might not dread opening the Bridge so much. After all, why hesitate when it can benefit both of us?

That seemed uncharacteristically reasonable of her.

I'll show you reasonable.

Her voice in his mind was too sweet. It made him nervous.

It should.

They were already at the top of the building, tying their rope to a decorative gargoyle dripping from the corner of the structure like hardened candle wax.

She was throwing the grappling hook before he could gasp.

I like these arms, she said in his mind as the hook clattered onto the roof of the palace, far across the moat. *With my old arms, I never would have made that toss on the first try – if ever. Keep this muscle up and we'll go far.*

Tamerlan's cheeks heated. Strange that they would still react to his emotions even though his arms obeyed only Lila. Etienne drilled him in sword work whenever they weren't hunting the

Grandfather. He wasn't close to good yet, but he was getting tighter, stronger, more disciplined.

Yes. And I like it.

Lila tugged the line one more time, satisfied at the tightness as she tied final knots on this side. She'd better know what she was doing.

It's harder with one eye, but I'm getting the hang of it.

Everything was harder with just one eye. He'd been learning that.

And here we go!

Before he could object, she slung a leg over the rope so that she was hanging upside down, gloved hands holding the rope, and boots sliding along it as she began to descend hand-over-hand from the height of the Court building to the Palace.

If he dropped…

If his arms were too tired or his hand slipped …

Queasiness washed over him.

Stop fretting. I can feel you trying to tense. I've done this a thousand times.

But he hadn't.

It doesn't matter.

Tamerlan let his eyes drift out over the dark city, studying the city braziers and the way they made patterned reflections over the canals like flickering lace. Following the lines of lanterns where people were busy Drawing Bounds, still celebrating this odd Autumngale holiday despite the heavy rains at harvest and the lines of refugees. How odd. How very human to cling to surface things as if they were the bones of their lives while the actual bones melted away.

And then they were on the palace roof, slipping through the shadows like the shade of a ghost. Lila found a door down through this defending outer shell and into the palace within like she'd been born in this place.

I practically was. Well – not my actual birth, but we thieves talk about our "births" to our new life as the time we made our first snatch. When I took the Portrait of a Young Man Named Avatar from this palace it was not my first snatch, but it was my first one that I was truly proud of.

So, she'd been here before! Did that mean she could find the library?

In my sleep, pretty man. In my sleep.

The palace was well-lit despite the late hour. And yet, Lila was hardly seen. Where she didn't slip quietly in the shadows, she walked with an unquestionable confidence as if she owned the entire palace. Night maids bobbed curtsies to her as they passed. Guards on the night shift made brisk salutes.

It was an epic deception.

Or it would have been.

Tamerlan was just beginning to breathe a sigh of relief when they stepped into the Library – a towering room filled with books to the ceiling and lit by the light of the moon filtering through a domed glass ceiling. But he was breathing too soon. A woman stood in the doorway of the Library. A woman holding a candle in a holder and dressed in a filmy nightdress and silk shell.

Her hand flew up to her mouth and she almost screamed before Tamerlan's hand joined hers and Lila grabbed her shoulder and pushed her against the nearest bookstack.

"Not a word or you're dead," Lila whispered in Tamerlan's voice and he shuddered at his words. If he could have said anything other than this, he would have.

There was only one other person who could make him feel so protective and so at home and she was locked in a clock in H'yi.

Let me speak! He begged the Legend. Please let me speak!

The moment his tongue was free he breathed her name.

"Amaryllis."

12: At Home in a Library

TAMERLAN

He pulled his hand away from her mouth, though Lila kept her pinned against the shelf with the other hand.

She opened and shut her mouth twice like she was afraid to speak before finally breathing, "Tam! Oh, dragon's blood, Tam! I thought you were dead. Our father – "

"I don't want to talk about Decebal." Lila was giving him the freedom to use his own voice though she kept control of his body looming over his little sister. "I want to know that you're okay. That you're not being hurt."

"Hurt!" she said it like it was a joke. "The only one who is hurting me is you."

Lila eased back slightly but she still kept Amaryllis in place.

"Do you want to marry this man? This Renli?"

Her eyes went wide. "Of course I do, Tamerlan. Do you have any idea … you don't, do you? Tam, they were going to sell me to be the Lady Sacrifice! If Renli hadn't stepped in. If father hadn't convinced him to marry me … I'd be dead right now!"

Tamerlan couldn't control the anger in his voice. "Father? Who do you think they were paying the sacrifice fee to?"

Amaryllis' lips tightened. "Don't be like that, Tam. I'm so happy to see you that I just want to think about happy things. For years I dreamed we'd see you when we visited Jingen and we never did and now here you are – in my home!"

"Your home," he echoed. The words felt like a slap. He was out there trying to fix things and save the world from sacrifices and risen dragons and everything and she was here making a home in a palace.

She laughed a tinkling, musical laugh. "My home with Renli, of course. We're marrying on the last day of Autumngale and then all of this will be mine. Father is so pleased, and of course, so am I!"

"Father is pleased." He sounded like a sailor's bird repeating everything she said.

She frowned. "Tam, don't spoil this. It's just nice to see you again. We had such magical times when we were children, didn't we? You and me playing together … before you went away?"

"I didn't just go away, Amaryllis," Tamerlan said gently. What was the point in raging against her? None of this was her fault. "I was sold. I was ripped from my home and sold like a stock animal. Like one of our blue bulls. And my family took money for my life."

She blinked back tears. "I know."

"And they would have taken money for yours."

"It's how things are. But I was saved at the last minute. By Renli."

"Who also paid a price for you. A bride price, but still a price."

Her frown deepened. "Renli loves me."

"Renli owns you. That's different than love. Come away with me."

She gasped. "I would never."

"You don't have to marry him."

She scoffed. "You don't get it, Tamerlan. I want to marry him. I don't care that he paid for me. Don't you get it? He saved my life. And why should I be mad at Father? He was just trying to help our family – like he did when he sold you. If he hadn't sold you, we wouldn't have been able to pay our debts to the Di'Sham family. He wouldn't have garnered us the favor that made all of this," she looked around her at the Library, her meaning clear, "possible."

Tamerlan felt the blood rushing from his face. If he'd had control of his body, he would have stumbled backward.

I think we've heard enough, don't you?

He would have died for her. And she wasn't even sorry that he'd been sold all those years ago. Not once she began to benefit from it. Horror filled him. And a betrayal that felt like a stab to his belly.

Lila took his voice and for once he gave it to her willingly.

"I wish you well then, sister. Many happy returns on your wedding and may your bond be blessed. Would you be so kind as to show me where your books on Legends are located? Surely you wouldn't deny your brother a chance to browse through your library?" She smiled charmingly with his lips. "I promise, I will put all the books back in place before morning."

His lips were still smiling as he released his hold on her and while Tamerlan's heart withered in his chest, Lila's words brought a familial smile to Amaryllis' lips.

"I knew you'd understand. And of course, you can look at the books. Just be sure to be gone by morning. Father wouldn't understand why I indulged you."

Indulged him? It was his life that made hers possible. First when he was sold. Then when he gave up the shreds of his life that were left to try to save hers.

Ignore her. Fools are a dozen to a half-copper. Use them as needed, then discard.

"I'll be certain to leave this place in order," Lila said with Tamerlan's voice before leaning down to kiss her cheek. Tamerlan wanted to close his eye. To stop the pain of kissing his sister goodbye with the bitterness of her betrayal still on her lips. Amaryllis. He would have died for her. He had been so certain that she loved him, too.

"Take the light," Amaryllis said lightly, handing him her candle. "I have no need of it."

"Good-bye, dear sister and may you find what you seek."

Maybe it was best that Lila was controlling him. He wouldn't have been able to force out those words. He fought against waves of sadness that threatened to steal his mental focus as Lila slipped into the library, never looking back when the library door shut behind Amaryllis with a click.

See? It's good when I'm in charge.

The light was a boon. They hurried along the shelves, Lila's fingers running along the spines of the books. But it was Tamerlan who felt a thrill of pleasure strong enough to temporarily erase the hurt of the last few minutes. This library was amazing. It had every volume he'd read or heard of on each subject. It was almost painful when Lila dragged his body past them but there was no time to stop and browse each one. No time to run fingers lovingly over the spines of familiar friends or delve into the first pages of books he'd never read before. No time to flip through, perusing the more interesting ones and making stacks of which ones he would read.

No time.

Here they were. The books on the Legends. His heart was racing quickly with anticipation.

Oh, look! He'd only ever heard of this volume!

Exploits of Cherrylocks stood out, the red leather of the spine enticing him. He tried to reach for it, but Lila stopped him.

Nice try, pretty man, but I think I'll keep my secrets from you for now.

Tamerlan's eye skimmed the shelves.

No books rumpled or torn or sticking out further than the others. Hmmm. No sign of dust disturbed, or parchments stuck in pages…

What was she doing? He was here to find books on Grandfather Timeless, or of anything that might trap a Legend.

Can't you tell he's been here? I can feel his residue like an oilslick in the spirit world.

Who's residue?

Grandfather Timeless. Now, concentrate and look for what is out of place.

But it was obvious which one the Grandfather had been looking for. Tamerlan had seen it immediately. *Queen Mer and the Sea* sat innocently between *Abelmeyer's Conquests* and *Orange Wars of the Dragonblood Plains.* That wasn't where it belonged. Those books were histories of wars, whereas the Queen Mer book was purely autobiographical. Anyone looking would have noticed it at once.

I didn't notice it.

Anyone who loved books would. It was out of place.

Lila snatched up the little book, riffling through the pages. Ah. That page was slightly torn. This was the book they were looking for. This was the one the Grandfather had been reading.

Are you sure?

It was the one.

Any librarian worth their salt would have noticed that as quickly as Tamerlan had and replaced the book. The change had to be recent. Maybe even earlier that day. This was the book that would give a clue to where the Grandfather had gone. Tamerlan felt a stab of anxiety slashing through him. And then what? Would they be able to track him down again? And when they did – how would they catch him when he could blink out of existence?

I don't think he's blinking out of existence. I think he's moving to a different time.

What, like he was suddenly ten minutes in the past?

Or twenty years. Or a decade in the future. Who knows? I'm not time. I've taken a lot from people – gems, gold, fine clothing. But I don't steal time like he does. I leave people with their days, their beauty, their memories, their health. The Grandfather snatches all of that – eventually.

Tamerlan shivered as Lila tucked the little blue book into his shirt.

They'd promised not to take any books.

And she was supposed to love you and be on your side. Consider us even.

What do you have to do with any of that, Lila?

I'm just restoring balance to the world. You're welcome.

And now they needed to find a book that would teach Tamerlan how to trap the Grandfather once they found him. They couldn't bet on beating him senseless. They needed some device, some amulet, some … something … that didn't require his eye.

Nah. We don't need that.

And then she was slipping through the shadows and back up to the roof.

We do need it!

She ignored his protests. Frustration filled him as he fought uselessly against her hold. She ignored his protests as easily as ignoring an itch, slipping through the palace like a shadow.

If it had been Tamerlan controlling his body, they would have been caught. There were so many eyes on him, so many guards watching, so many chances to mess up. But Lila seemed almost giddy as she slid past every palace defense and left her small candle in front of the last staircase like a burning bright flag. She tucked the little book into the front of his shirt, jamming it down behind his belt.

It's fun to be free – if only for a few hours!

Did Lila have an avatar somewhere, sleeping beneath earth or sea or in a clock?

I'll never tell!

Was that why she didn't want him to read about how to trap Legends?

There's no such book. There was only ever one true way – not the way of Abelmeyer's Eye, that's a temporary thing – and that way was never written down. Hopefully, it was forgotten.

If that was true, then what hope did he have? Maybe she was lying.

She was scrambling back up the rope in his body, ignoring the protests of his muscles as she climbed, hanging upside down. She'd better stick around until the climb was done! Tamerlan didn't think he could complete it on his own.

Isn't this your body climbing?

It was. But it wasn't his mind. This kind of thing took mental toughness as much as physical strength.

I'd say 'you're welcome' but I already said that.

She was the most puffed up creature on the planet.

I'm only being accurate.

But he still breathed a sigh of relief when their feet were back on the gargoyle and they were sliding back onto the roof of the Court building.

"And what were you doing in the palace, boy?" a gravelly voice asked in the darkness. It was like a knife sliding between his ribs as he realized just who was waiting for him.

Anglarok.

13: Meeting of Players

Tamerlan

When Tamerlan had been a child, he'd been the most afraid of the things that you found in the dark. The things you couldn't see that crept up on you. The things whose weaknesses you couldn't assess, because they were hidden. There was nothing good in the dark, because even good things morphed into terrifying things when the lights went out.

When he'd lost his eye, he'd lost half the light of the world. And here in the dark the sound of that voice cut him to the soul. He was cornered on the edge of the roof by an enemy. There'd be no daring escape here.

You forget that I'm in charge.

Lila spun him around. She was crazy if she thought returning to the palace was a good idea. They were caught between one side and the other!

But she wasn't listening to him. She was already scrambling along the rope, hanging down so that his head and back were to the canal moat below and his face was looking up at his hands furiously climbing. The rope jostled. He looked back. A knife glinted in the moonlight as Anglarok carefully sawed through the rope.

He didn't have time to scream – wouldn't have been able to anyway with Lila in charge. They were plunging through the air before he realized what was happening, swinging head down with the rope still clutched in his hands and the wind of their fall whistling around him.

He could see Jhinn's gondola below in the moat of the palace. He could see Jhinn there with his mouth open and a figure in the shadows behind him. He could see the moonlight glinting off the moat and the bobbing light of Jhinn's gondola lantern. They were going to hit the water of the moat. And it was going to hurt.

Pain struck him as hard as the water. It forced his breath out of his lungs. He released the rope, clawing his way to the surface of the cold water, pain and panic welling up inside of him. Would the weight of his sword and belt pull him into the clawing depths of the canal? And yet, it still wasn't him controlling his body. It was all Lila. Maybe she didn't find things so fun anymore.

I'm having a blast.

And then he was sputtering on the surface, sucking in as much water as air, the sword dragging him down in the water. Strong arms pulled him up from the drink just as Lila fled his body.

So long, pretty. Let's do this again.

Her timing was perfect. She'd left just before he leapt from the wok into the flames.

The woman holding him as he spewed out water and vomit had a single lock of dark hair hanging long over her harsh face while the rest was cut short. And the sharp expression on her face wasn't the only pointed thing digging at him. The tip of her sword blade nicked his throat.

"You're not as hard to find as you think you are," she said. "I wonder if you're even easier to kill."

This woman is surely insane, Byron Bronzebow said from his mind. Tamerlan couldn't have agreed more. *Try to charm her to get her on our side.*

Charm her? He'd be lucky to survive her.

Say something unbelievable, Lila suggested.

How would that help anything?

Trust me.

"I'm harder to kill than you might think," Tamerlan growled.

She laughed and the sword tip eased back just a hair.

Keep going. She'll respect bold words.

"If you really want to set Marielle free, then maybe you should come with me," he suggested. "Right now, I'm the only one who can free her."

"I'm listening," Liandari said, her look turning considering.

But now Tamerlan was panicking. That was the most outrageous thing he could think of. First, defiance. Then a suggestion that they become allies. What crazier thing could he say?

Tell her your plan! Lila urged.

But he didn't have a plan!

Then now is the time to make one up. Deathless Pirate suggested. *The simpler the better.*

"We will head to the sea," Tamerlan said, scrambling in his mind. After all, the Grandfather had been reading about Queen Mer. And that meant the sea. Hopefully, he hadn't lost the book in the fall. He thought he still felt it inside his shirt. "That's where Grandfather Timeless has gone."

Liandari smiled wider and she moved her sword back to threaten Jhinn who regarded it with as little worry as he would a dead fish. "Go get Anglarok, boy."

Tamerlan gasped as the sword left his throat, looking around him carefully. A dark shadow waved from the bank and Jhinn steered the boat toward it.

"I think you should trust me to guide us," Tamerlan suggested, "and I'll trust you not to try to kill me along the way."

Her laughter was echoed by Anglarok's as he leapt into the gondola from the shore.

"Well?" Liandari asked.

"He smells of truth. Why not give him a try?"

"Or I could kill him right here," Liandari said and the sword was back to threatening Tamerlan again. She was far too fond of that thing!

"That didn't work out for you last time," Tamerlan said. "And it won't work out for you this time, either."

He'd have to smoke more spices. Could he pull them from his sleeve and light them without tipping his hand?

"But then you'd never get what you want," a new voice said from the land.

Etienne leapt from the bank into the gondola, sending it rocking and Jhinn cursing.

"Watch it! If you flip it now, I'll lose the whole rig."

"What are you doing here?" Liandari asked but her sword was still at Tamerlan's throat.

"Looking for him," Etienne said, nodding at Tamerlan, but his eyes stayed on the Harbingers.

"Then why don't you ask him whatever you came to ask?" Liandari said. "I'll just keep my sword handy. And then when you're done, you can go. I have plans for this boy."

Etienne shrugged, but the way he stood seemed like he was tensed for something. "Did you find a clue to the Grandfather?"

Tamerlan hesitated. Shouldn't they deal with the people holding weapons on them first and worry about books later?

Etienne coughed. "Well?"

Liandari let the edge of her blade touch his throat again.

Reluctantly, Tamerlan pulled the sodden book out of his shirt handed it to Etienne. "See for yourself."

Liandari scowled as she watched Etienne take it. He snorted, opened it, and began to read. Someone had left one of the pages dogeared.

"And her avatar remains in the sea's embrace, awaiting the time of the return of Legends," he read. "The Grandfather goes to free Queen Mer?"

"Yes," Tamerlan said, hoping he was right. Anything to keep this chaos from spinning out of control.

"And these two?" Etienne asked. As if the Harbingers were Tamerlan's guests and not threatening him with blades. "What are they doing here?"

"I think you're done with questions now. Time to leave." Liandari twisted and her sword darted toward Etienne.

Etienne reacted so quickly that Tamerlan could hardly duck, parrying Liandari's testing thrust. She looked surprised as he pressed her back with the strength behind his blade.

"We want the girl," Liandari said as if she were negotiating. "She's the key to finding the one who opens the Bridge of Legends – the one who endangers us all. Why do you think that our people have returned? Why do you think we've come to your five cities?"

Little does she know, he's right here in front of her! Lila was laughing in Tamerlan's mind, but he didn't feel like laughing at all. He stepped back to where Jhinn stood with his paddle held at the defensive. Anglarok stood casually between them and Liandari. He wasn't fighting them, merely keeping them from interrupting his lieutenant as she tested Etienne.

"And I'm willing to spill your blood right now if it means getting the information we need to get her back," Liandari said.

"I don't have that information," Etienne said coolly as his sword met hers in a careful parry. The swordplay seemed like more negotiations.

"It sounds like it's in that book."

"Only if you know how to read it. Which you don't."

Think Tamerlan, think! They were hunting for him. They weren't afraid to use violence. They were heavily armed. This game Etienne and Liandari were playing wouldn't last forever and then they'd be tying him to a chair to torture him again.

There was nothing for it. He had to smoke.

He looked at Jhinn who raised an eyebrow and nodded emphatically. He was thinking the same thing.

Desperately, he pulled a roll of Spice out of the oilcloth pouch in his sleeve and ducked behind Jhinn to light it with Jhinn's gondola lantern. The roll lit immediately. He bought it to his lips, sucking in smoke as quickly as he could.

"You stay put!" There was tension in Anglarok's voice but it eased when he saw what Tamerlan was doing. "Those things are a filthy habit. I had a friend who got a big lump in his mouth from doing that. Grossest thing you ever saw."

Come on! Come on!

He'd sucked in too much smoke too quickly. He turned to the side and was noisily ill into the canal as the grunts and clangs of a fight continued above him.

Too late to worry about the fact that an entire fleet is after you. Just don't get caught, Deathless Pirate suggested as he snatched up Tamerlan's body. Easy for him to say. He was already dead.

"It seems your man doesn't have much of a stomach for violence," Liandari said to Etienne as they fought. "Maybe the same is true of you?"

He shouldn't be smoking again. He'd said last time would be the last.

It's better this way. Doesn't it feel good to surrender control? To let someone else take the reins? Even if it's just for a moment?

Deathless Pirate drew his sword, leaping to his forward.

Anglarok swung toward Tamerlan but the butt end of his harpoon hit Jhinn as he turned. The boy fell back with a cry. Deathless Pirate leapt over his fallen body, yelling a war cry as he slashed his blade aggressively at Anglarok.

"By the bones of my dead, I'll cut you down!"

The look of shock on Anglarok's face filled Tamerlan's vision.

Don't kill him! Don't kill him!

They didn't need another death on their hands.

No need. This is fun!

Deathless Pirate lunged forward, snatching Anglarok by the throat and lifting him up in one hand.

This had been a mistake.

Mind and will must be powerful. Know what you want! Calling me is never a mistake.

There was a cry of frustration from Etienne as Liandari battled him back to the ferro.

"Give me the book," she said.

Deathless Pirate tossed Anglarok overboard like unwanted cargo. He hit the water with a splash.

"Keep him from the boat with that oar, boy!" he called over his shoulder to Jhinn and then he was bouncing forward on the balls of his feet. He snatched Liandari up by the waist in a single armed hug, tossed Tamerlan's sword into the bottom of the boat and grabbed her wrist with his sword hand, grinding her wrist bones in his grip until her sword fell, too.

Behind them there was a loud *thunk* and a moan as Jhinn obeyed, prodding at Anglarok with the oar while he tried to keep his feet under him. He swayed as he stood – still recovering from the hit he'd taken. The second that Liandari's sword fell, Deathless Pirate grabbed her waist in both hands and hurled her into the canal.

"To the oars, boys!" he cried. "Pull for all you're worth! Pull, you ragged sails!"

There was a splash and a moan and then Deathless Pirate had an oar in each arm and was rowing so hard that Tamerlan thought he might tear the muscles in his shoulders. But it was good. It was so good just to ride this amazing power and capability - if only for a short time.

Etienne's jaw muscles tightened as he leaned down to get face to face with Tamerlan – a small action, but he had to be feeling the same pressure Tamerlan was. After all, he'd opened the Bridge before, too. These two were here to hunt him, too.

"I have affairs to attend here in Yan," Etienne said quietly. "This … interruption … hasn't changed that."

"We have bigger concerns," Deathless Pirate said with a grimace. "Unless you want your throat slit by that violent woman and her Scenter. Come with me. Let's go find the Grandfather."

Jhinn snickered in the back of the gondola. He must be okay if he was finding humor in this.

Tamerlan risked a look behind him to see two sodden people pulling themselves up along the canal. They knew he was headed to the sea. They wouldn't be far behind. Already, they were hailing another gondola as it slid down the canal. He heard the commotion as they demanded that it follow them.

"Of course, I want Marielle free," Etienne said. "But I need a few more days here to finish what I started before I go heading off on another wild chase."

"Not an option," Deathless Pirate said. "We are pursued by enemies. There is no time to stop to let you off."

Etienne made a frustrated sound in the back of his throat.

"Unless you want to swim for it." Deathless Pirate sounded gleeful at the suggestion.

"I'll stay with you," Etienne said curtly.

Behind them, the gondola took off quickly with Anglarok and Liandari in it.

"Then help me row, dangerous one," Deathless Pirate said. "We have enemies to outdistance. And a woman to save from a clock."

Etienne leaned in close. "I know that you're in there, Tamerlan, and when you resurface, I'm going to make you pay for this."

But he took an oar and threw his back into rowing as Jhinn stayed frozen in place at the stern, staring at their pursuers as he steered the gondola through the rainy canals under the light of the autumn moon.

14: GHOSTLY GUARDIANS

MARIELLE

If it hadn't been for the scent, she would have never found him. In this murky haze of souls forging their paths over one another, through each other, around each other, finding just one person was like finding the moment an idea was born. It was nearly impossible. But the scent propelled her on.

There he was! His scent filled her like breath, licking up and over the edges of her walls until she felt like she could melt in it. She moved toward the scent, feeling in the darkness of time and space until she thought she might almost be able to touch …

A specter rose up – beautiful and terrible. Her long red hair whirled around her as her hand thrust out and she hissed, "He's ours. Be gone!"

And then she was tumbling away, spinning through time and space again.

She needed to find him again. She knew now that she could. If she could find the scent she could follow it. But next time she would need a plan for dealing with the red-haired woman. Because she was beginning to forget and she desperately needed to remember.

15: Cogs and Gears

Tamerlan

The Yan Canal was a man-made channel formed years ago to keep Yan City connected to H'yi and Xin. It bridged the space between the Alabastru and Cerulean Rivers. Barges headed up the river, loaded with heaping cargos – oranges and seafood brought up from the sea for the Autumngale feast, timbers and stone to finalize summer repairs and projects before the cold of winter, thick sacks of grain and crates of dried fruits to fill the storehouses. Family boats floated in both directions, filled with laughter, squawking chickens, the clang of hammers working, and the quiet conversation of the boat nomad peoples. It was a picture of bounty and culture and of the ever-moving nature of life on the Dragonblood Plains.

Tamerlan glanced at Jhinn. Did he look at his people with envy? He didn't have a family boat to return to like they did. Most of the gondoliers had a gondola tied up to a family boat. None of them lived in their gondola like Jhinn did.

"I left that behind a long time ago," Jhinn said when he noticed Tamerlan looking. "My gondola is better. I don't need other people."

Tamerlan nodded. If the boy wanted to be alone, that was his business. Sometimes Tamerlan wished he could be alone – even if only in his own mind.

We only want to help you. The dragons must be stopped, and order restored, King Abelmeyer said in his mind. *As the only living person we have a connection to, we want to help you save our children's children.*

And how could he say no to that? But he was going crazy in the loudness of his mind. Crazy as he tapped his fingers along the gunwale of the gondola while Etienne slept in a heap of cloth at the front of the gondola. He should sleep too.

Was Marielle going insane inside the clock?

How did you know if you were losing your mind?

His eyes scanned the canal behind them constantly. He'd lost sight of their pursuers at daybreak – but it didn't mean that they weren't still there. He didn't have Deathless Pirate's superhuman strength anymore. And just plain Tam didn't have the strength to row like a machine. He should smoke again. He should let the Legends help.

"Tamerlan? Tam?"

He rubbed his eyes. He was vulnerable to them when he was tired. He needed sleep if he was going to hold off the constant temptation of smoking again.

"King Abelmeyer?"

Tamerlan looked up from the yellowed waters of the canal.

He blinked as he glanced at Jhinn's concerned face. "Oh, sorry. I missed that, Jhinn."

"You'll get her out, Tamerlan. And you'll find a way to calm your demons."

"Thank you," he said gravely, smiling at the younger man. He paused a moment before adding, "You don't need to keep transporting us, Jhinn. We can find another boat. You are too selfless, friend." He put his face in his hands. He was so tired. When was the last time that he'd slept? "I don't know why you stick by me when no one else cares."

Jhinn's face turned hard. "Because I couldn't help someone else – someone like you. He was a brother to me, but he roams the lands of the dead now. His spirit drifts like the winds. There should have been another way to save him."

"That doesn't mean that you owe me anything," Tamerlan said gently.

"And you don't owe Marielle anything. We choose who we'll care about. And owing people doesn't factor into that. Loyalty isn't about who owes who. It's about who you choose to tie strings to – who you choose to keep caring about even when no one else does. It's not about reciprocity. It's about … I don't know. But it's not about that."

Tamerlan was silent for a long time. He pushed away the voices, trying to drown them out as they responded.

You can use a person like that.

Loyalty is a commodity that can't be bought.

Give yourselves to the great cause!

That wasn't how he felt. He felt – humbled.

"I'm deeply honored by your friendship, Jhinn," he said.

"I'll ignore the things your demons say about me," Jhinn said with a sly grin. "They might be useful to me yet."

Tamerlan felt his cheeks grow hot. "How do you see them when no one else does?"

Jhinn shrugged, looking away. Maybe he didn't know why. Maybe it made him uncomfortable not to know.

Tamerlan tried changing the subject. "How are we moving so quickly?"

He'd just noticed that they were outpacing the barge next to them. And no one was rowing.

Jhinn snickered. "Remember that device you were helping me with? Look."

Tamerlan followed his pointing finger to where he was pedaling in the bottom of the boat. What in the world was that?

"It turns a gear that multiplies the power which twists a shaft that turns a propeller. And that propeller moves us forward with surprising speed. I'd thank you for it, but I'm relatively sure you had no idea that you've been helping me design this. Those ghosts of yours can be very useful if you catch them unaware."

He hadn't had any idea. He'd been obsessed with finding the Grandfather. His eyes widened. Had Jhinn been fishing the knowledge of this out of his mind without him even knowing it? He really was going mad.

"It will get us to Choan days faster than usual. We can even go upriver with it more quickly. Those demons won't catch us with this."

Tamerlan felt his cheeks heat. "I'm afraid that they're always with us. With me."

"I don't mean your ghosts, boy. I mean those Harbingers." Jhinn spat. "Devils. Both of them."

"And Etienne?" Tamerlan asked, amused.

Jhinn shook his head. "That one should have stayed in Yan."

"I don't think he had a choice," Tamerlan said. Deathless Pirate wouldn't have let him leave. A boat drifted by beside them smelling of the cinnamon tea that was so popular during Autumngale. His belly rumbled. "Do your people celebrate Autumngale?"

"Not the same way. Autumngale for your people is the time to remember the civil wars. For us, it was the time that Queen Mer chose us and made us alive. It's a time of creation. We celebrate by creating things."

"Like the gears and pedals on that device?"

Jhinn shot him a proud grin. "Yes. Isn't it beautiful? I can make more, too. When this is all over. But first we free Marielle from the lands of the dead."

"If you were smart, you wouldn't stay with us. You'd go off on your own and build those machines and live a good life." It bothered him that he was holding the other boy back.

"I'm smart enough, but life on the water can be boring. Life with you is not boring. I plan to stick around. Now, think, boy. How do you catch this Grandfather? Stalking him has proven useless. You need a trap, Tam."

"I know, but I can't think of anything, and I don't want to lose my other eye – not unless I have to."

"Catching the Grandfather is like trying to net a fast fish. You need to drive him into a set – into a net or trap he can't get out of."

"How do you trap a Legend?"

"With bait. Stop chasing him and let him come to you."

It sounded so simple, but he had no idea how to do it. "What can you use to bait a Legend?"

Jhinn shrugged. "Find something he wants. Easy."

But it wasn't easy and as the day wore on and they reached the Alabastru river, Tamerlan still hadn't thought of anything and he was beginning to think he could see that gondola in the distance upriver – following them. How long until it would catch them? And what would those Harbingers do if they ever caught up again?

The ruins of H'yi rose in the distance – partially burnt out buildings and blackened ruins. A gleam of light in the center of it might have been sunlight glinting off the clock. His heart lurched at the thought. She was just over there. It felt as though there was a string from her to him, pulling him all the time and the further away he went, the harder it tugged at him.

Two months hadn't been long enough for the city to be rebuilt after the fires. Not long enough for the population to be restored. Not long enough for plants to grow over the ruins of Jingen city on the back of the slumbering dragon next to the riverbank. He'd put that dragon there with his eye. But at what cost?

Was saving the world worth losing a person you cared about? Marielle had given everything for H'yi and no one even remembered her name.

He was still deep in his musings hours later as he took a turn pedaling the boat so Jhinn could sleep.

Just let us out and you can forget. Maid Chaos whispered in his mind. *I'll take you for a merry ride.*

You want to plan a trap? I'm the master of traps. We can start in H'yi. You want to go there, don't you? That was Lila.

He played with one of his paper rolls and thought about who might cross the Bridge of Legends and come to him. Their voices all the time were wearing through his resistance. Wouldn't be easier to let one out? Then he'd only have one voice in his mind, controlling his thoughts, driving him slowly insane.

"I hope you aren't thinking of doing that," Etienne said grimly, sitting beside him to look out over the devastation.

"Why haven't you jumped into the river and swum back?" Tamerlan asked a bit harshly. "If you had plans back there, you know I can – won't stop you now. You could just go."

Etienne hesitated. "I'm not sure there's any point to that now. Last night I might have changed her mind. But today … not today."

He was reading a slip of paper over again. With a sigh, he handed it to Tamerlan.

"I suppose there's no more point in keeping it from you."

E.

It's been a pleasure. But if you see no way to the future I want, then I see no way to the future you want. The Whisper withdraws our support. We'll back another.

A.

"'A' is Allegra," Tamerlan interpreted aloud. "A dangerous woman."

Etienne snorted. "That's like saying that the dragon Jingen over there is dangerous. It's true, but not true enough."

"What did she want from you?"

"Something I couldn't give."

Him, Lila said. *Trust a woman's intuition. That's bitterness in that note. She wanted him.*

Tamerlan watched his face. Watched the sorrow, disappointment and bitterness washing over it.

"When did they buy you for the government?" he asked bluntly. "Were you in your teens?"

"I was five when they bought me to be heir of Lord Mythos. I didn't even know what it meant. I wasn't even from Jingen. I was from Yan. I grew up with the Lord Fable as the legendary ruler of our city, not the Lord Mythos. They are the same, of course, but even the name was foreign to me. But they wanted a clever boy. Clever and malleable."

"I wouldn't call you malleable. Neither would Allegra."

"Well, that didn't stop them from molding me." The bitterness hung thick on his tongue. "For all the good it did me. My city ruined. My people destitute. They stand in line for bread. It hollows their souls."

"And Allegra won't help you? She won't use that secret organization of hers to back you in … what? Opposing Yan and Decebal in ruling that city? Is that what you wanted? Revolution?"

Etienne's eyes narrowed. He hadn't expected Tamerlan to guess, had he?

"Sometimes revolutions are necessary."

"Necessary for your people or necessary for you?"

"My people need me. And I'd give anything to help them."

"Except what Allegra wants?"

He flinched. "I didn't know she'd take rejection so poorly."

There was another long pause where the only sound was the sound of the gears whirring as Tamerlan pedaled.

"She's not the kind of woman who takes 'no' well," Tamerlan agreed. "How did you meet?"

"There are many skills you learn when they're grooming you to lead. You need to know every aspect of the city you will rule. You were surprised when I scaled a wall in the rain. That's a small thing compared to the things I was taught. One thing was siphoning magic from sleeping dragons – just enough to keep the city safe in small ways. Like holding off plagues. I met Allegra six years ago – when the old Lord Mythos ruled. It was the year that the Green Plague hit Jingen and Xin. Do you remember it?"

"Barely." He'd been bought that year. He came to the city months after the plague was gone.

"It was virulent and terrible. A man would sneeze and five hours later be dead in the streets. A child would go to bed whole and never wake. It haunted our cities. And Allegra was one of the Cure Mistresses fighting it. I was sent to help them with the authority and magic of the Lord Mythos at my disposal. That's how we met – destroying the plague. I knew what kind of woman she was almost immediately – the kind of woman who could do anything."

"Even foment revolution."

"Revolution is only the change of power. She could be a queen like Queen Mer. A Legend in her own right."

"You sound like you're in love with her."

"It would be crazy to love a woman like that. She would consume you alive."

Tamerlan chuckled. That seemed exactly true of Allegra. But he had a feeling that Etienne might like to have been consumed by her.

"And why do you have no apprentice of your own?"

"I should have one by now. But look at me." Etienne barked a laugh. "I'm almost as crazy as you are, Tamerlan. Hunting a Legend. Turning down perfectly good offers of power. Working with my enemies. I'm adrift on the seas of power. I can sense that a huge wave is coming, but no matter how I scramble, I can't avoid it and I can't find a way to ride it out. It will swallow every city of our Plains whole in a single bite. And there's nothing we can do about it."

"Nothing but keep fighting."

He laughed – a cynical laugh. "Do you know how the dragons first came to the Dragonblood Plains? They came from the mountains. The dragonblooded were fighting amongst themselves and in their fighting, they created a terrible weapon. And once it was created, they could not defeat it. They fled their mountain homes to these plains. They married the people here. Lived with them. Mixed blood with blood. Until one day when the dragons followed them. And all their sins came home to roost. What can we do to avoid the terrors we have wrought? What can we do to avoid the fates we've twisted for ourselves? If anyone could do that – well, he'd be saved. Saved. Don't we all want to be saved?"

Tamerlan felt his eye burning at the thought of that. If there was one thing he wished he could be, it was saved. Saved from the voices. Saved from the guilt. Saved from the waves that tossed him back and forth like driftwood.

"What kind of trap will hold the Grandfather?"

"The clock held him," Etienne said.

"But what kind of bait would tempt him? I don't like your plan to give up the rest of my vision to sedate him. I think we should try something else first. I think we should set a trap and wait for him to trip it."

"Now, *that* is a very good idea. It will require some thought."

And they sat together and listened to their demons as they raced to follow the twists and turns of the river.

16: Lies and Rumors of Lies

MARIELLE

He loved bunnies. He was cooing to them as his father spoke in the background. He seemed too old for that – fourteen maybe and his full height though a little gawky, but the sweet expression on his face as he tended them made him look younger than he was. Azure faintly tinged him with the scent of aspens – gentleness.

"He'll be fine for the Alchemists. He's clever. He reads. Valuable. You'll be happy you paid such a low price for him."

He was trying not to listen, that was clear, as he put them back in their hutches, petting each head and offering green plants to them. It was a goodbye. And the sad swirls of wisteria scent that spun around him mingled with his golden warm honey and cinnamon scent and drew her in. She wished she could comfort him. Wished she could help him. Wished she could draw every thread of that wisteria purple from him and cast it away until he was all golden beauty without this thick wrapping of sadness.

He flickered. And then he was in a gondola beside Etienne and they were both staring at the sleeping form of a dragon, half-buried in mud. And he smelled just as sad in the boat. Puffs of wisteria filled the boat and drifted behind him down the river.

A spirit that looked like a King shot up from his form, ghostly and pale blue.

"You're not welcome here," he said to her, authoritatively.

She gasped. He could see her? Then the red-haired woman had not been a mistake at all. There were spirits claiming Tamerlan.

"He's mine," the ghost said.

He flicked a finger and she tumbled away, rolling through history and time. She was standing in the swirling snow beside a man wrapped in rags, a sword in each hand and a wild look in his eyes. A cage stood beside him, door flung open, and inside it, a single shell lay. It pulsed turquoise with magic. The man licked his lips and then the vision was gone and Marielle tumbled back into the whirl of time.

17: CHOAN

TAMERLAN

"And how are we going to get through that?" Tamerlan asked as they passed the city of Choan on one side and the city of Xin on the other bathed in the orange beams of the setting sun. Gulls swooped and called as they ended their day and the hurry of barges and riverboats grew more pronounced as they rushed to arrive at their destinations before the sun finally set.

But for Tamerlan and his companions, the night had just begun.

Beyond Choan, the Retribution fleet had drawn closer, until it was almost upon the city. White sails filled the horizon. And it was through those sails that they would have to pass to get to the Isle of Mer.

He read the passage about Queen Mer for what must be the thousandth time.

Queen Mer stays to guard us still and her avatar remains in the sea's embrace, awaiting the time of the return of Legends. For she was placed among the arms of the sea and in the embrace of the tide she was set. She was honored on the Isle of Mer and enthroned in majesty there until the Day would come once again.

It seemed clear enough. Queen Mer's avatar was somewhere on or near the Isle of Mer. And the Grandfather was headed there for some unknown reason. What did he want with her? And was this the kind of bait that Tamerlan needed to set a trap for the Grandfather?

Bait is something you put in a trap before your prey gets there, Deathless Pirate reminded him. *This is not your bait. Turn your mind away from the thought.*

But if he could find out why Grandfather Time was so set on pursuing Queen Mer, then maybe he could figure out what he wanted. That was how you found bait – understanding what your prey wanted …

We should stick to the original plan, Abelmeyer argued. *Stalk the Grandfather and catch him. All this business with traps and bait is too much like Ram the Hunter. It will drive you mad.*

The problem with having voices in your head was that it was hard to formulate plans when they kept interrupting all your thoughts with objections. And for that matter, if Queen Mer was a Legend, why was she never in his head?

Because she's never won the right to steer your body, Abelmeyer said. *She's been preoccupied with other things.*

Tamerlan shivered.

A barge of oranges floated by, heaped high and full with the round fruit and set on delivering them into the city. The

Retribution flotilla hadn't stopped the orange ships. How strange. With them waiting there like a dragon waiting to leap on its prey, you'd think they would stop them, but the delivery was here, just in time for Autumngale.

Around the barge, a small skiff floated by, carrying a group of refugees. It was easy to recognize the hollow-eyed looks of people who had grown used to the idea that there was nothing left for them but ashes. These must be people from H'yi still filtering into Choan. Perhaps they had tried to survive for a time in the ruins there. Usually, Byron Bronzebow would be clamoring in Tamerlan's mind – but he was oddly quiet.

There had to be some way to help all these people. There had to be some way to rebuild the lost cities – Jingen and H'yi and bring back the prosperity they once had.

"No one else cares," Etienne said, looking at the same boat. His mind was in the same place as Tamerlan's. "I want to make everything safe again, but no one else cares. Oh, they say that they care. You should hear your father wax eloquent on the matter in the balls Yan has been hosting."

"What are you doing attending Landhold Balls, Etienne?" Tamerlan asked, pedaling past the skiff. He didn't want to think about his father. He'd avoided the man's public appearances assiduously.

He threw his irritation at the thought into pedaling. The pedals made them faster than any other boat on the river, and yet that gondola behind them was still gaining. His mouth formed a thin line as he looked over his shoulder to see it in the distance.

It was always there. Always shadowing them. What magic could make it as fast as Jhinn's little device?

"I've been searching for cracks. Looking for ways to restore balance. The Five Cities are important. They must be restored, and the people kept strong. You aren't the only one with the ability to hide in the shadows."

"Looking for ways to gain power again, you mean," Tamerlan said bitterly. "That is, until you scorned Allegra."

Etienne shot him an angry look. "I'm here with you right now, aren't I? Does this look like I'm grasping at power?"

Tamerlan shrugged, but it couldn't dislodge the guilt. "Sorry."

Jhinn's snores in the bow of the boat continued unabated.

"How will we get past that blockade?" he asked, still pedaling. They might be at odds in their view of the world, but they still needed each other to catch the Grandfather and put him back in the clock.

Etienne was watching the slowing traffic. It was down to orange barges and family boats now. Every reputable boat had scurried to safety as darkness descended.

Tamerlan lifted the coal in its small cage, planning to light the gondola light behind him but Etienne threw up a hand.

"Not yet," he said. "Wait."

He was tense, watching the boats.

"The flotilla lets the orange boats through. They stop fishermen and other traffic, but they let the orange boats through."

"Sure," Tamerlan said, but his eyes were drifting back to the gondola following them. Was it his imagination, or had they sped up again? How were they doing that?

"It makes sense to blockade us from the sea. To weaken the cities by stopping trade. It makes sense if you are waiting to scoop them up when they grow weaker."

Now, he was certain of it. The other boat was gaining on them. Tamerlan felt for his sword. It was still there. And for his rolls of Spice. He'd need them too, if they were overtaken.

"Which means they are biding their time," Etienne mused. "Do you know how many oranges we use every year in the Orange Wars, Tamerlan?"

"I have no idea."

And he didn't care. Every year fools took perfectly good oranges and threw them at each other in mock wars that imitated the civil wars – the real Orange Wars. Every year people wandered the sticky, citrus-scented streets the next day with black eyes and broken noses from mock fights that got out of hand. No holiday in the Dragonblood Plains was hotter for the gambling community. There were bets on injuries and wins and losses and even though it was all pretend and meant nothing, those chalk lines actually did make a difference in the cities. If your side won, there were connections made, trade deals, respect from your fellows and that insubstantial currency subtly influenced your status and wealth. The Orange Wars on Autumngale were foolish and dangerous – but they did mean something.

But he wasn't thinking about Orange Wars. He was trying to gauge when he should smoke his Spice. Darkness was descending. Every moment made it just a little harder to see. And with the gondola lights unlit, he had to dodge empty barges going back out to sea to unload ships beyond the blockades and full orange barges headed back to the city. Why didn't Etienne want the lights lit? Perhaps he thought they would lose their pursuers in amongst the traffic?

"Thousands. But it's better than actually killing each other. All those resentments and angers and disputes spill over into what has become a yearly sport – a war where territories are fought for and claimed by the throwing of oranges until one side or the other gives up and goes home. All they win is bragging rights. And yet it works. It commemorates our civil wars – and it prevents more civil wars."

It was more than that. Even Tamerlan knew that, and he was pretty sure that Etienne did, too.

"That's nice," Tamerlan said as Jhinn stirred in the front of the boat.

"I think that what we need to do," Etienne said, "is leave this fine gondola in Jhinn's capable hands while we take one of those barges to sneak past the blockade. And we need to do it quickly. Because when the Orange Wars start, I have a bad feeling that it will be more than oranges flying this year."

Tamerlan looked up. Was Etienne saying that the Whisper was going to act this Autumngale? The Orange Wars would be the perfect cover for a revolution.

Tamerlan opened his mouth to ask if Etienne, but at that moment, Etienne launched himself over the side of the gondola, leaping onto the deck of an empty barge beside them.

"What ho, good captain!" he called as Tamerlan cursed, jumping up from the pedals and Jhinn woke.

"That boy is crazy!" Jhinn said, yawning as he spoke.

"We need to leave you with the gondola," Tamerlan said hurriedly, checking his sword, knife, cloak, belt pouch, rolls of spice – did he have everything?

The gondola was gaining on them. He only had moments to make a choice.

"Can you wait for us in Choan? I need to go with him," he said to Jhinn and as the boy was still nodding, he leaned down, lit his Spice on the small brazier they kept to light the lanterns, and pulled in a draft of smoke.

"I'll be under the Jowl Bridge every night at sunset until you join me again!" Jhinn called as Tamerlan leapt up from the gondola, following Etienne into the dark. "And I'll watch for you. Where Chaos reigns, that's where I'll find you."

They shook hands in the darkness.

The gondola was nearly upon them and they'd just lost an ally in Etienne's scramble. He'd better hope that he'd secured them a ship. This was all going way too crazy, way too quickly!

And I'm here to save you from it all. Trust me.

"Go!" he called to Jhinn and he leapt from the gondola as the Legend took him.

18: At Sea

Tamerlan

If you could have chosen someone to take you over – you'd choose Abelmeyer. He was noble and brave and incredibly skilled with the sword.

Plus, I'm used to operating with just one eye!

He sailed with Tamerlan's body over the rail of the barge like he did this every day.

Muscles and bone and nerves that flash with life! It's a heady feeling! Let's rule this world!

His sword was out, flashing in the light of the barge lanterns as he struck a noble pose to the horror of the barge workers.

"We're being taken! Our ship is being stolen from beneath us! Raise the warning!"

Feet thudded on the decks and Etienne shot Tamerlan a furious glance, but it was Abelmeyer who spoke with Tamerlan's voice.

"STOP."

As if compelled, the sailors froze mid-stride.

"Your barge is hereby needed in service of your cities," Abelmeyer declared. "You will be compensated for this inconvenience and you will be sent back on your way as quickly as possible."

"You can't take the barge. We're hired out for the week!" The captain looked aghast. "As I was saying to your man here."

Etienne's scowl deepened. He didn't like being thought of as anyone's servant.

"And as I was saying," Etienne said. "It will only take you a few hours out of your way. We need just one stop at the Isle of Mer."

And what did he think they would do after that? Without a ship or boat, they'd be stuck there.

Our enemy will have transport. We will take it for our own.

And what if he didn't have 'transport'? What if he'd made a deal just as foolhardy as ours? What if he had others with him and they kept us from taking his boat?

You ask too many questions. Act. Don't doubt. Do you want this or not?

He wanted it.

You called me. Now trust me to do the job.

If Tamerlan could have clenched his jaw while Etienne finished the negotiation with the barge captain, he would have. But

Abelmeyer had other ideas. He strode to the stern of the ship and peered out at the gondola following them.

Where was it? It had been back there only a moment ago.

Abelmeyer whirled, scanning the people on the deck, looking in every direction in the river around them.

Where?

Etienne strode over, smiling slightly.

"Despite your hotheaded foolery, we've been given what we asked for," he said.

But Abelmeyer wasn't listening. He was looking. Searching.

There was a creaking sound from behind them and Abelmeyer spun lightning-fast bringing his sword up.

He was just in time.

One blade met the other in the clang of steel on steel.

Liandari was lightning fast, her blade snaking out like a viper in any direction that he wasn't guarding. But Abelmeyer was quick, too, turning her blade and spinning in a complicated movement that locked their swords together and almost succeeded in wrenching her sword away.

He pulled back from the clash, crouching low and darting his blade out like a flicking tongue of a lizard.

Flick toward her face. She countered.

Flick toward her feet. She danced aside.

Flick toward her wrist. That time his sword bit flesh.

But he didn't stay still. He leapt from the crouch and strode forward so quickly that Tamerlan's breath would have caught in his throat if he was the one doing the breathing. He pushed past her faltering guard and grabbed her throat with one hand, lifting her up and shaking her.

Beside him, Etienne was calling something, but Abelmeyer's ears were roaring, his vision reddening in his battle rage.

A hand was placed on his shoulder and he spun to look at whoever was touching him. Liandari shook in his grasp as he moved.

Anglarok stood with hands raised, disarmed by Etienne but it was Etienne who had placed a hand on Tamerlan's arm.

"Enough, brother," he said with a taut expression. "No need to kill her."

The red began to clear from his vision, but it wasn't Tamerlan who spoke. It was Abelmeyer.

"They are Banished Ones. The spawn of Queen Mer."

"We could use them to get around the blockade," Etienne said easily. "The barge is good, but what if they search it? These are their own people. They could help us get through."

"Help us or *betray* us?" Abelmeyer asked. "Their ancestors fled the five cities during the Orange Wars. How fitting that they would return during the Autumngale celebration when the Orange Wars are remembered. Have you forgotten that they chased us all the way here? They want our blood. They do not want to help us."

"We want Marielle," Liandari gasped. Abelmeyer set her on the deck, but he still held her throat. "We need her to track the opener of the Bridge of Legends. He is our doom. He must be stopped."

A muscle clenched in Etienne's jaw and Tamerlan flinched internally. Would he reveal that Tamerlan was the one who had opened the Bridge? Didn't he need Tamerlan as much as they did? Maybe that would keep him from being too honest.

If he does, I will dispatch them quickly. We dare not risk you.

"Does that mean that you will work with us to find Grandfather Timeless and set Marielle free from the clock?" Etienne asked.

"We have considered your tale," Liandari gasped. "About the clock. About the Grandfather."

"Give her a little breath, Tamerlan," Etienne said, leaning forward like a hunting dog.

Abelmeyer let go of her throat. But his hand whipped out to grab her sword wrist instead. She flinched as his grip bit into her wound. But she hadn't dropped the sword. That took discipline. Someone that disciplined might decide to strike at any moment.

She will strike us down the moment we no longer serve a purpose to her. And if she finds out you are our bridge to this world, she will do worse than kill you. We will not allow that.

How did he know?

Queen Mer sent them away with prophecies. Prophecies that the opener of the Bridge would destroy the world.

Well, Tamerlan wouldn't be destroying anything. Except for maybe the Grandfather.

Exactly.

Although, opening the Bridge of Legends often had consequences he didn't anticipate.

They are insane. Religiously insane and that is worse.

"We will help you find this Grandfather. Our quest is too important not to use whoever we can," Liandari said.

"She was trying to kill me a moment ago," Abelmeyer objected. "That's not the work of someone who wants to be an ally."

Etienne waved a hand dismissively. "I'll take their weapons. You can watch them. They won't cause trouble when we both want the same thing, will you, Liandari? We could use allies. The two of us haven't succeeded yet. Maybe if we were four, that would change."

It doesn't matter if he brings them along. One wrong look and we'll cut their throats.

That seemed harsh.

Would you rather they cut yours?

Liandari looked at Anglarok who shrugged and handed Etienne his short sword and harpoon. "Take them. But we would prefer if you guarded us."

"Why?"

"The boy smells of madness," Anglarok said, looking at Tamerlan as Tamerlan took the sword from Liandari's hand. He hadn't relaxed his grip on her wound. "The insane can be used, but never trusted."

Tamerlan felt Abelmeyer's jaw clench and he agreed wholeheartedly. He wasn't insane. Was he?

Always, the weak see the strong as mad. Visionaries. Leaders. Seers. Through the ages, they are branded as madmen. You are only thought to be mad because you have tapped into the rushing river of time and plucked out the Legends leaping through the water like salmon. You have birthed us into the world for a short time to feed your vision. Ignore the mortal.

"I think it's better if I watch them," Abelmeyer said calmly to Etienne. "The ship's crew needs your ability to calm them."

He nodded his head toward where the ship's crew was gathered around, jaws dropping open as they watched the tableau in the stern.

Etienne cursed softly and then nodded to Tamerlan.

Liandari grunted in protest, but with her weapons gone she could only protest with murderous looks.

"Don't kill anyone while I'm gone," Etienne said quietly – and he was deadly serious. He strode away, speaking calmly to the sailors like a man trying to reassure a dog, but his fist clenched and unclenched betraying his own worry.

Tamerlan smiled at Liandari and Anglarok, shuddering inside at the feeling of that smile. When Abelmeyer smiled with his mouth, it did not feel pleasant. It felt vicious.

"If we're really going to work together, then we need to talk," Liandari said as Anglarok opened his bag and brought out a roll of bandage for her wrist.

"I suppose you'll want to lay the groundwork for how to use me," Abelmeyer said with Tamerlan's voice. But Tamerlan was secretly cheering him on. Yes! She deserved to know how much that had stung.

"We're hitched together now – you and me. We want the same thing," Liandari said, her eyes hard as flint.

"Then swear to me by the salt of the sea and the salt of your blood that we are one until the purpose is met."

What did that mean?

It is how these people swear. If she does not agree, then she plans to betray us.

"How do you know about that?" Liandari's eyes flashed with suspicion.

"Don't try to guess how much I know."

Sometimes Abelmeyer sounded noble. Sometimes he sounded like an arrogant fool.

Don't insult the person who can destroy your body.

Liandari and Anglarok looked at each other and then at him. Their expressions were identical – narrowed, suspicious eyes.

"We don't make promises to the insane."

Abelmeyer leaned in close – so close that Tamerlan wondered if he planned to kiss her.

I'd rather kiss a snake.

He was still gripping her wrist as Anglarok danced nervously from foot to foot.

"Insane or not, I'll split you from navel to nose unless you swear."

They exchanged another dark look before they spoke in unison.

"We swear on the salt of water and blood not to try to kill you until together we have freed Marielle from the clock."

Abelmeyer gave them a small, tight bow. Confidence almost dripped off of him.

"I swear by the salt of water and blood not to try to kill you until together we have freed Marielle from the clock."

He sheathed his sword. What was he doing? They looked like they might try to kill him at a moment's notice.

Not now that they've sworn.

Anglarok spat and his face was dark with suppressed anger. But he took his sword from the pile and sheathed it, leaning his harpoon against the rail of the ship.

"The failed ruler has a way with words," Liandari said, nodding to where Etienne had calmed the ship's crew and got them back on course.

"A ruler only fails if his people die needlessly," Abelmeyer said, taking her wrist in his hand. "This needs stitches. Let me help you with that."

With a piercing expression on her face, she handed him a small oil-cloth packet and let him begin the work of stitching her skin. But tension and violence crackled in the air around them like lightning about to strike.

And if they ever realized that he was the one they were really looking for, then no vows in the world would save him. He'd just have to keep smoking and keep Abelmeyer there until they found the Grandfather. Otherwise, he'd be as vulnerable as a fish in a net.

I'll make sure you are safe. Just keep me around so that I can.

19: OUT OF REACH

MARIELLE

She couldn't help it. His scent drew her like a bee to a flower and now she was here, watching him again. Watching his blue eyes filling with wonder as he traced the structure of the Queen Mer library with his gaze. He was sketching it on a recipe page he was holding that was meant to make a stronger steel. But around the edges of the recipe were charcoaled sketches of the library. Of a child's face with the light hitting his eye at just the right angle to make it sparkle mischievously. Of an old woman's gnarled hands.

Tamerlan's smile was far away as he added to the collection of sketches.

"Tam!" Dathan is in trouble again!" a voice called to him, shaking him out of his reverie. "He bet against a blacksmith in cards and if he loses again, he'll pay with more than coppers!"

Tamerlan stuffed the pages in his belt and sprinted after the other boy.

That's who he'd been before all this. A dreamy artist. A thinker. A helper of friends.

But could you really say that was still who he was? After everything he'd done? She wasn't sure. But she was beginning to think she knew him now, or at least knew who he had been before he woke the dragon.

And yet, she felt a pull to him. She couldn't help but watch him wade into the tavern and push between his friend and the hulking blacksmith.

"Can I help you, friends?" he asked mildly.

"Only if you can pay his debt!" the blacksmith cursed. "Fool bet with nothing to back it!"

"I can pay you later," Dathan started, stumbling a little as he tried to step backward. His eye was already swelling – a red flower on his pale face. He must have been hit before Tamerlan arrived.

But the blacksmith lunged at him and Tamerlan had to throw a shoulder into the blacksmith's chest to hold him back.

"Whoa, whoa," he said gently. "No need for violence. It's not the answer here."

"He stole from me! And no one steals from Chysander."

"Chysander is it?" Tam asked with a friendly smile. "How much does he owe you?"

"Two full silver."

Tamerlan reached in his purse, pulling out two silver coins and holding them out to the blacksmith.

"Not enough, now!" the man sputtered, refusing to take them. "Now he's caused me trouble, too."

Tamerlan paused, the muscle in his jaw jumping as he considered what to do. "And if I take him away from here and offer you our sincerest apologies?"

The blacksmith muttered something, snatching the coins away and Tamerlan hustled his friend out the door. Dathan stumbled as he walked. He was mumbling as they went.

"I just hate feeling like I'm nothing. Hate feeling like I owe everyone and can never get out of it. I was sold. Sold like a pig for market. I'll be paying that back all my life to get free. All my life."

"I know," Tamerlan said, wrapping an arm around him to support his friend. Compassion bloomed around him in puffs of lavender scent.

"You, too. Sold. You can't go anywhere you want or do anything. You've got to work for the guild 'till they're paid their price. All your life."

"I know."

"What are we if we can be bought and sold? What are we?"

"We're friends," Tamerlan said mildly. "Or at least I think we are."

"You're a good friend, Tam," Dathan said thickly. "That was six month's pay you gave for me. How are you going to buy anything extra now? You'll have to live off guild bread and clothes from the lost bin."

"I'll live. And so will you. As long as you don't bother any more blacksmiths."

And that was why she was drawn to him. His sweet heart. His innocent love of beauty. His immediate willingness to open his heart and help a friend. He wasn't like her. He didn't think about right or wrong. But he cared about people.

She saw him. The real him. And it was hard to be against someone who you could really see.

She spun away from the intensity of the scene before her, following the thread back, back, back to the present. This time, she wouldn't let the king spin her away from the scent of warm honey and cinnamon.

20: Isle of Mer

Tamerlan

This place has changed, Abelmeyer said as they left the small rowboat from the barge. He was as tense as Tamerlan, every muscle bulging and ready for action. The smell of salt and wild winds swirled around them.

In the dark, the Isle of Mer was hard to make out beyond jagged rocks and an unforgiving coastline, but Abelmeyer seemed to remember it. The burden of being driven by someone else was wearing on Tamerlan, but that hadn't stopped him from smoking again a few hours ago, nursing the paper roll of spice as he leaned over the rail of the barge. Oddly, it seemed that it required his volition to do that. Abelmeyer hadn't been able to do it himself.

He hated that he was doing this. It felt like a kind of surrender to let the Legend take over his whole self. And he was letting him. That much was obvious. It wasn't Abelmeyer who drew out the Spice and lit it and smoked. That had been Tamerlan –

his only act of free will since he'd given over his body hours ago, but it was still *his*. And somehow that made it worse.

It was his choice.

But what other choice did he have? He'd tried to save Marielle in Jingen, only to have the city destroyed beneath them. He'd tried to redeem himself by saving H'yi and stopping the dragon the next time – and that had mired her in eternal imprisonment. She'd been right about that. He couldn't redeem himself. He wasn't even trying to anymore. He just didn't want anyone else to suffer because of his choices. Not Marielle. Not Jhinn. Not anyone. And that meant smoking. It meant turning over his body to the Legends and letting them do all the things he was powerless to do on his own. Was that surrender, or was that volition?

Anglarok kept glancing over at him with suspicion in his eyes. Could he smell the magic as Tamerlan drew it in?

It turned his stomach to think about all the ways this could go wrong. But if he didn't take the gamble, then nothing would go right, either. He would just have to hope – with what little hope he had left – that he could turn this around and somehow undo some of the tragedies he'd woven.

Sweat beaded on his forehead from the strain of his thoughts and his belly twisted with the sharp pains of a mind troubled by worry.

You destroy yourself from within. Learn to accept what can't be changed. We are your only hope to turn this around. The more you fight us, the harder it will be to fix your mistakes.

It would certainly be easier just to accept it all and surrender.

You can trust me to guide you.

And Abelmeyer hadn't done anything wrong in his body. He'd helped him stop the dragon Jingen. He'd made a pact with the Harbingers rather than destroying them.

Yes.

So why did Tamerlan feel more and more knotted up inside as the hours of his possession passed?

Be calm. We are almost at our goal.

The passage on the ship had been uneventful. It should have been terrifying. The ships loomed high and sleek on either side as they passed between them. Tamerlan had been shocked at their size and height – like giants looming in the water- far taller than most buildings in the Five Cities – and carried together on the peaks of each foaming wave. Their hulls were outlined by strings of lights in the night. Calls, bells, and whistles spoke of a precise schedule and a disciplined crew.

He'd been surprised by the air of alertness on the ships. Despite the darkness of night, they seemed ready to spring into action at a moment's notice.

"Are they always like that? Ready to pounce?" he had asked the Harbingers.

Liandari had answered him. "They are ships of Queen Mer's Retribution. We are proudly ready for anything."

Of course they were.

Anglarok's nose wrinkled as he scented from the rail, but he had watched in silence as they slid between the high ships. Tamerlan felt a creeping sensation as he played with the roll of Spice between his lips. There was something going on with these ships. They were not just waiting at anchor that night. There was a feeling about them like they were going to move. He didn't believe that they were always like this. And he didn't believe that they usually let barges slip between them with so little fuss. The ships had waved the barge through without even an inspection.

He had drummed his fingers on the rail, deep in speculation.

Etienne came to stand beside Tamerlan with a furrowed brow. He had a lit lantern which he held high in one hand while the book Tamerlan had found in the palace library of Yan was held in the other hand. He'd asked for it an hour before and his eyes had been glued to the pages ever since.

"Did you read something that troubled you?" Abelmeyer asked in Tamerlan's voice as he puffed out smoke.

"Filthy habit," Anglarok muttered. If he had any idea what Tamerlan was doing … but fortunately he didn't. If he smelled magic, he still wouldn't know what Tamerlan was doing with it.

Etienne's lips thinned as he pressed them together. He gave Tamerlan the same look every time he glanced at him. Etienne clearly didn't like interacting with the Legends. But would he prefer that he had just regular Tamerlan the apprentice swordsman at his side or the great King Abelmeyer at his side?

Don't let his reluctance trouble you. He doesn't know what a great gift you give him.

"The section with Queen Mer was not the only section he looked at in this book."

"How do you know?" Tamerlan asked.

"I read the rest of the book – something you should have done."

"Just explain, if you please," Abelmeyer said crisply with Tamerlan's voice.

"The section about Byron Bronzebow has a burn along the side of one of the pages – like it was held too close to a candle flame. A librarian would never do that. Only a person flipping through a book illicitly in the dead of the night would do that."

"Why is there a section about Byron Bronzebow in a book entitled *Queen Mer and the Sea*?" King Abelmeyer's voice sounded taut. Why was he so anxious about Bronzebow?

"It mentions off-hand that there was a tribute to him set up after the death of the queen and that there are similarities to their graves."

Tamerlan felt his hand tighten on the rail of the ship. What had Abelmeyer so upset? His knuckles were white.

"We'll worry about that once we've checked on the Isle of Mer," his voice said. But there seemed to be some added weight to Abelmeyer's words – like he was choking on them. "One thing at a time. Always, one thing at a time…"

He sounded crazier than Tamerlan felt and Tamerlan was the one with a whole party of Legends on his mind.

I am not crazy.

And now here they were, hours later, stepping out onto the Isle and it worried Tamerlan that he could feel Abelmeyer's heart racing in his chest like it was trying to outrun his feet.

We're here for the Grandfather. Be ready.

It felt so personal to Abelmeyer.

Isn't it personal to you? We wouldn't be here if it wasn't.

That was true.

"Prepare yourselves," Abelmeyer said, holding a lantern high above his head as they leapt from the rowboat the moment it was close enough to the beach.

Down the beach, a small sailed craft leaned precariously where it was anchored out from the shore. Waves had beat it into water too shallow for it. No one stood on the small deck. Etienne had been right. The Grandfather had brought a craft of his own.

That was never in question.

It was for Tamerlan. He didn't share Abelmeyer's unshakable confidence. Besides, what kept him from simply vanishing and appearing like he did last time Tamerlan tried to grab him?

That takes an enormous amount of energy and power. Without the reservoirs of the clock to draw on, he is limited in how often he can do that. Why waste it on the mundane?

"I smell trouble," Anglarok said and he held his harpoon at the ready while Liandari drew her blade.

The idea of them behind him with blades made Tamerlan's skin crawl, but Abelmeyer was unaffected, drawing his own sword and holding the lantern higher as they climbed up and around the jagged rocks.

"There's a shrine here somewhere," Etienne said, looking at the book in his own lantern's light.

"More than a shrine," Abelemeyer said calmly, but there was a sharp frost to his tone that puzzled Tamerlan. Had he and Queen Mer been friends?

Of course not.

Then why the horror tinging his tone?

Some things should never be done. And yet – sometimes they have to be.

The clock. The dragon. Marielle. That was his list.

We all have a list.

They clambered around a black rock that jutted up to the sky like a broken incisor, and then around two more. They seemed almost like a double-spiked crown.

"Inside the Crown of Mer," Etienne read from his book. "The arms of her ancients are frozen. They reach for the sky in horror at what was done to their Queen."

"Does anyone come here?" Abelmeyer asked quietly.

"Of course not," Etienne replied. "It is forbidden. The island is cursed."

And that didn't worry him? He was as mad as Tamerlan was!

There was blood on the rock in front of Abelmeyer. Someone must have cut themselves on the broken shards.

"So that boat had to be the Grandfather's then," Abelmeyer said. "But whose blood is this?"

They turned the corner and if Tamerlan had his own body he would have been biting back a scream. As it was, Etienne gasped and Liandari's jaw clicked as if she had shut her mouth hard over some response.

"Mer's spit!" Anglarok gasped.

This was the shrine.

It was set in a gap in the spiky black rocks. Arms had been carved reaching up into the sky – arms of the largest squid a person could imagine. Though if the book was to be believed they weren't carved at all, but frozen there - reaching in wavy desperation toward the sky.

"The Kratoen," Abelmeyer breathed, awe in his voice.

But the others weren't looking at the kratoen. They were looking at the dead girl hanging from a rope tied roughly to one of the arms, head down, her blood still dripping out of her into a sticky pool on the floor. She was the age of Marielle – or Amaryllis. Had she been as foolish as his sister, trusting the Grandfather only to have her blood spill on the rocks?

Tamerlan's soul shivered. This was what Etienne was going to do to Marielle. What he'd done to other young girls before. He shot a glance at the other man, but Etienne's face was stony and expressionless.

"Just your type of party, isn't it?" he said.

Etienne's dark look spoke volumes in the light of the lanterns.

"Do you see what it opened?"

And he was right, of course. The blood was pouring into a small channel cut into the rock. And a clam shell had been opened high above them – so high that whatever it might contain could not be seen from here. Steps led up to the opening. And on the steps, footprints were smeared in fresh blood.

Abelmeyer craned his neck, but he would have to climb the steps to see what was going on in the clamshell.

Beneath them, the ground trembled. Was it Tamerlan's imagination, or had one of those tentacles moved slightly? Abelmeyer swallowed, but he strode toward the steps without hesitation.

"Now we prove we are heroes," he whispered to the others. "Stab your knife through your courage and pin it in place lest it vanish with the meeting of blades."

Before they could answer, he was sprinting up the steps, sword in hand, lantern held high, ready to take on whatever he found there.

21: King Abelmeyer

Tamerlan

He stumbled at the top of the stairs, sword tip wavering. Was he shaking? King Abelmeyer shouldn't shake. He shouldn't stumble. Tamerlan was trying to see what had thrown him, but the King's eyes were looking everywhere else.

They were in a massive, black clamshell with runes carved along the rim. White pearls crunched underfoot – more pearls than he could have imagined. You could buy that whole Retribution fleet with this many pearls. You could buy a nation. They twisted under his feet, making ankles and calves work doubly hard to keep his footing.

All around them, music filled the air. An ethereal, haunting tune sung from unseen lips.

Abelemeyer – hands shaking, sweat dripping into Tamerlan's eyes – finally looked back toward the center of the shell, where the Grandfather stood wearing a tall top hat and long open coat. He was grinning triumphantly and draped in his arms was the ethereal half-there, half-not corpse of a woman. Her long hair fell around her, tangling in shells and chunks of coral like seaweed. Her blank eyes stared. But falling from her slashed throat was not blood – but more ghostly white pearls.

Not a living woman then – but what?

An avatar.

Her crown fell from her head, bouncing over the pearls and clattering to the edge of the shell at the same time that Liandari lunged forward toward the Grandfather.

"Defend yourself, Legend, or taste my blade!" she cried.

Shaking himself, Abelmeyer sprang forward, too, his sword darting toward the Grandfather like the tongue of a snake.

They needed to use the Eye to trap him. Now!

Laughter rolled over them from the mouth of the Grandfather as the music swirling around them began to fade.

He dropped the corpse of the avatar, dodging backward to put his back at the hinge of the shell. So little care! As if she did not matter.

Undaunted, Liandari leapt over the dead avatar, ignoring her too-pale skin and open mouth. But Abelemeyer couldn't step over her. Tamerlan felt him trying to move his feet, struggling against the impossibility of it.

Use the Eye! Tamerlan's thoughts were a scream.

Abelmeyer's gaze was fixed on the woman. The avatar.

Queen Mer.

Was it possible to kill an avatar? To destroy a Legend forever?

Yes!

And with that panicked cry, Abelmeyer fled his mind like a retreating army. And with him left the knowledge needed to use the Eye to trap the Grandfather.

With a roar, Tamerlan leapt over the cold form of the Legend queen. He wasn't spooked by the death of the dead. He wasn't worried that he might be mortal – he always had been. He shoved the cacophonous voices from his mind as the Legends' voices poured into his mind.

Dead? She can't be dead!

Have you seen her? Where is she?

Mer? Mer!

Abelmeyer, explain what you saw. Quickly!

Someone grab the boy again!

He mentally shoved them aside with a roar, slashing his sword toward the Grandfather as he battled Liandari blow for blow. The Grandfather laughed, turning Tamerlan's blade aside easily. Why had Abelmeyer fled at just the moment that he needed him?

"Two against one, is it? And yet you have no idea. I set you free. I kill your killers, destroy your destroyers. I release you from their power. Bow to me, fools!"

He sounded insane.

But who was Tamerlan to speak of insane? He could barely think with all the voices in his mind.

Why did you let go of him!

Fool!

You'll ruin us all!

Who was the fool? What were they talking about?

Etienne and Anglarok's voices rang out with concern, but he couldn't focus on that. The Grandfather was winning. He was going to beat Liandari at swordplay even though she darted and rolled like a ship on the sea, quick as a darting fish, but skillful as the fisherman. She sucked him into a false thrust, only to slide to the side, ducking under his guard and striking out with her knife. But beautiful and capable as her fighting was, she was not fast enough. Each blow just missed the Grandfather. When she moved to strike, he simply wasn't there.

Someone needed to grab him before he darted away. Like he had all those times before. Maybe they couldn't use the Eye to trap him, but they could hold him physically.

Tamerlan clenched his jaw, dropped his sword to the ground and leapt forward in the air, arms out, reaching for the Grandfather. All the Legends in his mind were screaming at him. His own fear was screaming at him. But someone had to stop that maniac. Now. Before he destroyed the whole world.

He felt cloth in his hands. Smelled the spice on the Grandfather's breath. Saw the gleam in his eye.

And then he hit the ground hard, scattering white pearls all around with his rib-cracking landing. His hands were clenched around something. He opened eyes that had shut in response to the fall.

But there was no one else there. Just a top hat clutched in his hands.

He scrambled up, scattering pearls all around him.

Spun.

Looking, looking, ready.

Liandari stood with her sword out and her jaw hanging slack like she'd been stunned. She closed her mouth with a sudden click of her jaw. Etienne and Anglarok were frozen in place, identical looks of shock on their faces and weapons held ready with no foe in sight.

"He vanished," Liandari breathed. "You went to grab him, and he vanished."

"And what about the woman who bleeds pearls?" Anglarok asked quietly.

"Queen Mer," Tamerlan gasped. He turned the hat around in his hands, staring at it as his heart sank. They'd been so close. So very close. He had the Legend's hat. "Her avatar is dead."

"They can be killed," Etienne said with a sound of horror – or was that hope? – in his voice. His eyes met Tamerlan's. They'd seen another avatar before – Deathless Pirate's. But that was all the way back in Xin.

"Mer's Spit!" Anglarok looked shaken, his dark face pale in the lantern light.

Liandari was muttering what sounded like a prayer. Her eyes were closed as her fingers tapped out a pattern on her other forearm. She'd sheathed her sword and her expression as pained – her face tattoos dark in the moonlight – as if they somehow were more significant now.

"We can set a trap for him," Tamerlan said to Etienne. He was trying to stay calm. Trying not to throw up with nerves and withdrawal. Everything in him wanted to smoke again – to call a Legend to help while he still could. Before they were all gone.

Call us! That was Lila Cherrylocks. *Trust us!*

"We just have to guess where he'll be next," Tamerlan said, swallowing down bile. The Harbingers looked like someone had killed their nearest relatives and the power of their emotions washed over him like waves of sound, reverberating in the echo chambers of his mind where the Legends screamed for release.

Etienne was quiet for a long moment, staring at the broken avatar lying in the sea of pearls at their feet.

"The Catacombs of Choan," he said at long last.

"Catacombs?"

Etienne met Tamerlan's gaze, hope and fear warring in their depths.

"They were long known as the haunt of Maid Chaos. Her devotees still go there on pilgrimage. It's the nearest place belonging to a Legend that I can think of."

"But will her avatar be there?" Tamerlan wondered aloud. In truth, he didn't want to go there. He shivered at the horrific memories that flooded over him at the thought of Maid Chaos. The horrors she had wrought with his body – the people she had killed. He swallowed.

Etienne was shaking his head. "How would I know? I didn't know that the Grandfather's avatar was in that clock in H'yi. Didn't know about your pirate friend until we saw him through the glass. Didn't know about this shell. I don't think it's been opened since it was sealed. Or these pearls wouldn't be here anymore."

Tamerlan looked around him. He hadn't thought of that. But Etienne was right. No one would have left such a fortune behind – even if the island was said to be cursed.

"You're right," he agreed. "We have to hurry. I don't know how he left here, but if he can jump to another place as well as another time, he might be there already."

"It's not a trap if you don't get there first," Anglarok spoke, his words heavy. "And it's definitely not a trap if you have no way to catch the one you're trapping."

"We have a way, if Tamerlan will use it," Etienne said quietly.

"It didn't work. I tried but it didn't work," Tamerlan admitted. His face felt hot. "Do you have a better idea?"

Exhaustion filled him like water in a bottle. He didn't have any idea. Didn't have any books to read to get ideas from. He was just responding now, no longer initiating. He ran a hand over a weary brow. What else could they do? They could chase. They could try.

But what if the next Legend refused to use the Eye for him? He didn't know how to use it without them.

The only thing he didn't dare do was give up.

"We'll sail to Choan," Etienne said firmly. "And by the time we get there, you'll figure out how to *make* that necklace work."

"And the blockade?" Tamerlan asked wearily.

"That's Liandari and Anglarok's job – to get us through."

Liandari's eyes snapped open at her name, as if they'd shocked her out of her prayer.

"Enough talk," she said. "The worst is over. The Queen is desolated. We will bury her properly in these pearls and sail. And pray our souls are cleansed by salt and scoured by wind and somehow saved."

"Let it be this day," Anglarok agreed.

Tamerlan was silent. But he followed the others as they laid the ghostly, broken avatar in the center of the shell and covered her in pearls. It seemed like something a person might do in a dream – not something anyone would do in reality. But then again, who hunted down ancient Legends come back to life? Who made allies of enemies and fought wars to save the world?

His heart was heavy as they took to the sailing boat. While Etienne and the others prepared to sail, he found the bow of the boat and curled up in the "v" where they prow cut through the water and examined Abelmeyer's Eye. It was still the same as the day he'd found it. The fire hadn't harmed it. But then why hadn't Abelmeyer used it? Was it broken? Had they lost their chance? Nothing made any sense. He had the tool, but no way to use it. He let the darkness of despair wash over him until sleep stole him blessedly away.

22: Scent of Gold

Marielle

She found him as he slept, his eyelashes lying across his innocent-seeming face. Ghostly figures formed a ring around him, trying to hold her back, trying to prevent any contact. But she was not governed by them. She'd learned that, finally. Time and place had no hold on her. She slipped between them, to his side.

"Tamerlan?" she said gently, leaning in close to his sleeping form. She lay a spirit hand on his shoulder.

He muttered in his sleep, brow furrowing. And then his scent was there – swirling through her mind with intoxicating sweetness. Warm honey and golden light, cinnamon and tarragon, hot butter, and heat that made her want to open herself to him.

"Tam, can you hear me?"

He looked up at her – still asleep, but awake at the same time, meeting her in his dream. She almost melted at the pleased look in his blue eyes. Was she crazy? Hadn't she been certain she should avoid him at any cost? And yet, after seeing everything – after learning him so well, she couldn't hold herself back.

She needed to get a grip. She'd come to warn him, nothing else.

"Beware of the Legends, Tamerlan. All is not as it seems."

"Marielle? Is that really you?" he tried to sit up, but his body didn't respond – couldn't since he was still asleep.

She lay down on the ship deck beside him so he could look into her eyes. It felt so intimate – as if they were sharing a secret.

"Tamerlan, you have to watch out for the Legends."

"I'm going to get you out of the clock, Marielle. I promise." The tortured expression on his face nearly broke her.

He was trying to reach for her. She saw his hand twitch wildly as his sleeping mind tried to force his body to work.

"That's not important," Marielle said gently. "What's important is that you listen. You have to stay away from the Legends, Tamerlan. Whatever the cost. They want to destroy you."

"I'm sorry. I'm so sorry, Marielle. I should have saved you. I shouldn't have chosen to bring down the dragon."

He wasn't hearing her. He was too obsessed with taking care of other people. And wasn't that how he'd been his whole life? She shoved gentleness aside, making her voice firmer.

"You did the right thing. The just thing. But this isn't over, Tamerlan, and if you aren't careful, they'll use you. They've been using people all along."

"I shouldn't have left you in the clock."

Couldn't he hear her? It was almost as if he was speaking to her without hearing her words. Frustration filled her as she tried harder. Could he at least see her?

"Please, Tamerlan!"

"Shouldn't have left you, sweet Marielle."

His eyelids were drifting closed.

She clenched her jaw in frustration.

"Please, please listen! Stay away from the Legends!"

His eyes closed. She reached out to touch him and was shoved roughly away by a woman with swirling, ghostly red hair.

"He's ours, little Watch Officer. Go play law someplace else!"

She lunged for the other woman, but something caught her from behind pulling her back just before the woman with the red hair planted a fist right in her mouth. Her mind swirled, her vision darkened, until all she felt were blows.

They had him in their grasp. He was their tool, their plaything. And they had to be stopped.

She leapt to a different time.

23: Orange War

Tamerlan

He woke with a start, his hands grasping for someone who wasn't there.

Marielle.

Had she really been in his dreams? He'd felt her there – felt her as if she had really been present. He must be going mad.

In the back of his mind, someone was laughing. He didn't even know who.

"Are you awake, Tamerlan?" a quiet voice asked.

Tell him yes.

"Yes," Tamerlan muttered.

"Stay low," Etienne said.

Ask him if you are close to the next avatar yet.

"Are we close to the next avatar?"

Why was he doing what they told him?

"No," Etienne said. "Look up – but look up carefully."

They were sailing into Choan, their deck loaded with oranges. Etienne must have met a barge along the way and filled the boat with their cargo. Why hadn't Tamerlan woken up for that? He must have been more tired than he realized. He wished he could remember what Marielle had been trying to tell him. She'd been so beautiful – so pure – like a fresh wind blowing through a muggy city.

They weren't alone.

Mist rose off the canals and the river as they slid into the first lock of the Chaon canals. It wisped up in ghostly flickers around dozens of other orange-laden boats. In the greyness before dawn, something flickered on one of the barge decks like bright metal catching the light inside the heap of oranges. Maybe someone was hitching a ride like they were with this cargo. Maybe other sailors had stowed away among the round fruit.

People gathered solemnly along the canals, receiving oranges from the barges and loading them silently into barrows or carts. It was as if the citizenry were haunting their own city. One woman's eyes were dead as she took her wheelbarrow and started off. Another man's face was drawn as he went through the motions of checking a manifest list against the contents of the barge.

Why participate in the celebration at all if they felt so grim?

Tamerlan had never been fond of the Orange Wars reenactment on Autumgale. Despite the toothsome scents that wafted from the open windows of people's homes – ciders and baked gourds with cinnamon, stewed fish and cakes of crab – despite that, there was violence to come. It would be mock violence. Not many people died from being hit by an orange – but still violence. He usually tried to find a quiet corner and stay hidden with a book until the Wars were over and the sticky streets calmed. Something under Tamerlan's skin crawled at the thought of that violence today.

Their boat shoved through the canals toward the Alchemist District of Choan.

"A strange thing, this celebration of yours," Anglarok said from his perch beside Tamerlan. His eyes were on the orange barges, studying them. "Your Lord Mythos says that every year, the people here reenact the Orange Wars and every year it becomes more and more about the fun of throwing oranges and winning territory from your neighbors to brag about and less and less about remembering the thousands of people who died long ago in the real civil wars."

"It's true," Tamerlan said, staying low like Etienne had asked, but easing himself into a ready crouch, checking his weapons and kit as he got ready to leap from the ship. He put the chain of Abelmeyer's Eye back over his head, tucking it into his shirt. The ruby had given up none of its secrets. All he could hope for now was a miracle. That or outright incapacitating Grandfather Timeless.

"He says that in one of them – the last one if the stories are true – enemies hid on a boat of oranges and infiltrated the cities. That brave act was the catalyst for this celebration – the reason that so many oranges flood into the Dragonblood Cities every year and the reason that you throw oranges in your mock fights."

"Yes," Tamerlan said. His sword and knife were ready. He was ready. When they got to the catacombs, he wouldn't let the Grandfather slip away this time.

"He says the mock fighting will begin at dawn."

"Any moment now," Tamerlan agreed.

"Strange that they don't check the barges for more than oranges."

It was strange. Tamerlan's brow began to furrow at the thought. IT reminded him of something. Something hidden. Hadn't Marielle been saying something about that?

She was never here. That was only a dream.

But even still …

"And will these people be ready to fight real enemies, or is it all a game?" Anglarok asked. There was a knowing spark in his eye. Tamerlan tried to pull his mind back to the conversation. Did Anglarok know something that Tamerlan didn't?

"It's a game. A violent game, but only a game," he tried to be reassuring. "We'll be doing the real fighting in the catacombs."

"Etienne says those are under the Alchemist District. He says they can only be accessed through the Embalmer's Guild."

"It's news to me," Tamerlan said. "I had no idea there were catacombs here. You'd think they would flood."

"You would think so. They must use effective pumps," Anglarok said, his eyes still on the barge. "Is that it?"

He pointed to a large white building along the canal with a black tile roof that seemed too large for it. Round windows speckled the building like a black and white goat on a ridge. A large sign over the main doors read, *Embalmers' Guild of Choan City*.

"Seems to be," Tamerlan said, his eyes on a patrol of the City Watch as they marched along the canal between their boat and the guild. They were so precise. So certain of themselves. Marielle would be like that if Summernight had never happened. Or she'd be with these Harbingers if she hadn't ended up in the clock.

He should be looking for Jhinn, too. He was here somewhere, waiting for them. And he had the rest of the Spice. If Tamerlan kept smoking the rolls he had in his sleeve, he would need that soon. He was down to ten rolls. That wouldn't get him far if he needed to keep calling the Legends.

He felt nervous just thinking that. As if he'd already decided to call them. But that Bridge hadn't been crossed.

Yet.

There was a strange movement in the barge beside them. The oranges were tumbling from the deck into the canal and bobbing on top of the water. What -?

Anglarok sprang to his feet before Tamerlan could clamber up to his. Liandari rushed to the front of the boat, leaning on the railing and peering up the canal.

The first golden ray of dawn lit the edges of the buildings, washing over tile roofs like a blessing from the heavens. Something glinted in the dawn light on the nearest orange barge. Hadn't he noticed a gleam there before?

A roar of voices filled the streets of Choan as dawn broke and people poured from their houses, unleashing waves of thrown oranges at each other. Like the tide let loose it all happened at once. Yells of triumph and cries of pain filled the air.

An orange sailed through the air toward their boat and Anglarok speared it casually with his harpoon, pulling the fruit off the end of the blade and peeling it enough to take a juicy bite.

"A waste of good fruit."

Their boat bumped up against the edge of the canal and Tamerlan wavered a little.

In the boats. They're in the boats. One of the voices of the Legends broke out from the mass of them talking over each other. *The boats!*

He glanced at the nearby barge. Oranges were falling off the side still, dropping in the canal to bob in the water there. But that was no surprise in this chaos. The street above was crowded as Etienne leapt from their sailboat to the canal edge and began to pull the boat in by its rope.

"We have to hurry!" he called over the chaos. "This is only going to get worse!"

Moments ago, Tamerlan would have never guessed that so many people were waiting to break out of their houses, but now the canal rim was packed. One man tried to dodge a flung orange and lost his footing, falling with a curse into the canal water and bobbing below the dark surface with bright oranges all around him. There was a laugh from his opponent above – barely audible over the cacophony of voices above. Someone shouted a cheerful cry, but it wasn't all goodwill above them. More than one eye sparkled with malice as an orange was flung to hit a man from behind.

Juice – sticky and fragrant – was already spilling from the edge of the street into the canal as Liandari and Anglarok disembarked, joining Etienne on the shore.

"We have to get to the catacombs!" Etienne yelled over the roar of voices. An orange hit the wall beside him, splattering against the rocks and sending a mist of juice over him.

He scowled and Tamerlan barely bit back a laugh. Etienne could use being hit by a few oranges. The man had such a high opinion of himself.

Maybe you should give it a try.

He almost scooped up an orange before he stopped himself. Wait. Had those thoughts been his, or Lila's? He'd never had a problem with Etienne's pride …

Shaking his head to clear it, Tamerlan leapt from the boat to join the others on the ledge and scrambled to follow Etienne as he hurried towards the nearest steps up to the streets.

The Harbingers were distracted, looking constantly at the orange boats as if they expected them to produce dragons out of the oranges like hatching eggs. Liandari tripped, catching herself on the rock. She needed to watch where she was going!

Tamerlan's mouth formed a firm line, but they were almost to the steps now. Etienne seemed distracted, too, as he drew his sword and Tamerlan pushed past the Harbingers to join him in the front, drawing his own sword to use as a threat as they forced their way up the steps, pushing the orange-throwing citizens up in front of them.

"Make way!" Etienne bellowed. "Make way!"

"What's troubling you?" Tamerlan said as they crested the last step, holding their place until Liandari and Anglarok slid up behind them.

"Today, we were supposed to take Yan," Etienne said calmly. "If Allegra hadn't withdrawn her support. It could have brought hope for my people. A second chance. I'm missing it."

"A civil war?" He didn't know why he sounded shocked. With the fall of Jingen and the burning of H'yi, this should seem like a normal thing. Nothing was shocking anymore.

"Sometimes we must do what we must."

Interesting. His father thought he had all the power in Yan right now, and yet there were ways he could be toppled. It would be as easy as …

His thoughts were interrupted by a growl of approval from Anglarok and he followed the man's gaze to where a new burst of voices roared together in a single war cry.

"Retribution!"

Oranges flew in every direction as they poured from the barges floating in the canals. Not one or two or three people, but hundreds of men and women in loose trousers and long vests, their arms and necks and torsos tattooed with coastlines and maps. They waved harpoons in the air, pouring onto the canal ledges and shoving up the stairs violently.

"Did you know?" Etienne asked, whirling to confront Liandari and Anglarok. "Did you know about this?"

He sounded hysterical. There wasn't time for this.

"No time!" Tamerlan yelled, grabbing Etienne by the upper arm and dragging him toward the buildings on the other side of the street.

Wars would have to be dealt with later.

One thing at a time.

Exactly! Abelmeyer was right about that.

Screams erupted around them as people fled, slipping on smashed oranges and falling under each other's feet. Doors slammed along the street, barring access to any but their own. Behind them, shrieks of horror filled the air with the clash of steel and the cries of injured and dying.

Oranges were no match for real weapons.

And the Retribution would be on them in a heartbeat if they didn't move.

Tamerlan plunged toward an alley as Etienne continued to question the Harbingers.

"Are you with us or them now that the attack has begun? I must know if you'll stay the course!"

"We swore on blood and water," Liandari growled. "We will help you trap the Legend."

But Anglarok was watching his compatriots with longing, stealing looks over his back as they flooded over the streets.

Tamlerlan clenched his jaw and ran down the alley, leaping over people scrambling from building to building, trying to return to their homes.

"Find shelter!" he roared at them. "Find weapons. You're under attack, you fools!"

A seven-year-old boy ran toward him in the alley and Tamerlan scooped him up, practically throwing him up the steps of a nearby home.

"Inside," he yelled. "Get inside!"

The child darted inside the door. Whether it was his home or another, he would be safer there than the chaos of the streets. Tamerlan paused for a heartbeat, torn over whether to say with the child but with the Grandfather loose in Choan, worse things than invasion might happen and he was the only one capable of stopping the Legend.

Had he just thought that or had that been the voices in his head?

The light at the end of the alley bobbed in front of him and a sense of pulling drove him toward the white building at the end of the long, dark alley. The Embalmers.

He pushed every ounce of power into his legs and ran. Bursting out into the street into a hell of flying fruit, stampeding people and screams. Tattooed invaders rushed down the street, flinging people in every direction so that ruined bodies and smashed oranges mingled in a stew of blood and acid.

Crouching low, Tamerlan held his sword at the ready, Etienne moving to cover his right side.

"Those are my people," Liandari shouted over the chaos. "You can't stick a blade in them!"

"Then tell them not to kill us!" Etienne roared back as a harpoon smashed into his sword.

"Retribution! By the salt, I'll have your hides!" Liandari roared. "Back, you mob of crabs! Back!"

Her shout didn't stop the charging man right in front of Tamerlan. The man lowered his harpoon and rushed toward

Tamerlan. If only he'd smoked! If only he had someone else controlling these amateur arms of his!

He brought his sword into place just in time to deflect the attack, pushing with his blade to push the harpoon to the side. His enemy pulled back only to lunge again as Tamerlan leapt to the side, grabbed the haft of the harpoon and pulled, flinging his blade tip in front of the other man's chest just in time to pull him into the blade.

His gut twisted within him as the man's face crumpled in pain.

"No time for that," Etienne yelled, tugging at his arm as Tamerlan fought to free his blade from his enemy's ribs.

Somehow, Liandari had broken through the assault, carving a way to the doors of the Embalming Guild.

Tamerlan yanked his sword free, sliding and slipping after Etienne, not daring to look at his feet, not wanting to see that it may be people and not oranges he was stumbling over.

"Hurry," Anglarok said. "I smell worse to come!"

They reached the doors and Etienne wrenched them open, stumbling inside. But Tamerlan wasn't sure if he should be more worried about what was within or what was without. Outside was invasion, violence, and death. Inside, was the Grandfather – probably. Or, at the very least, Maid Chaos' avatar. And either one of those made his bowels feel like water.

24: Chaos Born

Tamerlan

Come on! Come on! Kill! Maid Chaos' voice broke through the chaos in his mind.

His head was aching so hard from all the voices that he felt dazed. Pain sliced through his mind at the louder voice cutting over the rest.

I can feel the avatar. She is close! Hurry!

And there's more, Lila Cherrylocks interrupted. *I feel Choan stirring.*

No time for that! Maid Chaos again. *Focus! Focus!*

Dragon. Ram was always focused.

If they were lucky, she wouldn't already be dead. If they were lucky.

The Grandfather is with her. You must be ready.

That meant he had to smoke. Tamerlan stumbled along behind Etienne, holding his head in one hand, trying to think. Could there be a downside to smoking?

Open the Bridge! Do it! Or you'll be too late.

Last time there hadn't been a downside. Abelmeyer had performed wonderfully. It felt wrong to rely so much on the Legends, but when he smoked the chaos was gone, the voices silent – except for one. He would be able to think again. But Abelmeyer hadn't been willing to use the Eye. And this time, they needed to use it.

Clamor filled his mind as the Legends urged him to listen, making thought impossible.

Let us guide you!

We will help!

Open the Bridge!

You need us right now. We can fix everything.

Of course we'll use Abelmeyer's Eye!

"I smell something strange below," Anglarok said. "Something beyond embalming spices and blood. And it must be powerful to drown those out!"

Open it!

Anglarok pulled out a shell from his pocket, placing it to his ear.

"It's here somewhere. Something … wrong."

"Then we have to hurry," Liandari said, looking back at the door they'd barred behind them. "The invasion is succeeding. This building won't be empty for long."

They all looked nervous. But to them, the chaos was without, and to Tamerlan the chaos was within.

Let it end. Open the Bridge. I will take your hand! Abelmeyer called to him.

Let me out! Lila Cherrylocks insisted. *You know I can help you! I will use Abelmeyer's Eye for you!*

My avatar! My avatar!

Tamerlan clutched his head, trying to hold back the pain of their screams.

"There must be a way down," Etienne muttered, running his hands along the wainscoting on the wall as Liandari perused the shelves upon shelves of spices.

"This is for the dead?" she asked. "But why is there no one here?"

Etienne shook his head. "I don't know. But I see no doors to below, only steps to the floors above."

"I smell the dead everywhere," Anglarok said with his nose wrinkling. "But there is something more."

He sniffed along the wall, following his nose like a hunting dog. Tamerlan felt a pang of sadness at the sight. He looked just like Marielle.

And she'll never get out of the clock unless you let us out!

Nothing else mattered compared to freeing her. He was past redemption, but there was still hope if he could only free her.

It was his choice to make. And his choice was Marielle.

He took a roll of Spice from his sleeve. This wasn't the time to be fussy. He needed to open the Bridge and let out a Legend before they found the way down. It was his only hope to use the Eye and trap the Grandfather.

There was still a fire burning in the hearth. He plunged the roll into the fire and lit the end.

His hand was shaking. He wasn't ready to go blind. But what other choice was there?

"Here it is!" Anglarok said, pressing his fingers to the carved edge of the wainscoting. The floor beneath them began to slide and an opening formed with steps leading downward.

"Come on, Tamerlan," Etienne called, catching Tamerlan's eye and shaking his head at the Spice.

Tamerlan hurried to follow, but he kept the roll of Spice at his side. Etienne might disapprove, but they still needed the Spice. They needed the Legends. They needed all the help they could get. No matter the cost to him.

He hurried down the steps behind Etienne and the Harbingers, nearly stumbling over Anglarok as the man fell to his knees, clutching his face. Moaning in high pitched agony as he tried to cover his nose and mouth from whatever smell was below.

No time for that.

Tamerlan leapt over Anglarok's crouched body, hurrying down the steps. Below was the Maid Chaos's avatar, and the Grandfather would be there – he was sure of it. If he did this right, they would save Marielle at long last.

25: Stalking Madness

Marielle

She'd followed them from a distance. They didn't seem to notice her unless she was close, but they buzzed around him like bees, their ghostly selves flickering in and out of sight as they stalked him. His head was in his hands as if he were trying to block them out, while around him they each tried to whisper into his ears.

Maybe out in the real world they might look grand or noble, but to Marielle, the ghosts of the Legends looked like gnarled, twisted spirits. Their translucent appearances winked in and out, elongating to stretch toward Tamerlan's ears as they spoke incessantly to him.

Let us out! Let us out!

It was a wonder he wasn't mad!

Or maybe he was. Maybe that explained a lot.

She felt a twinge of pain – or was it fear? – at the thought of Tamerlan going mad. It felt deeply personal, somehow.

He was fighting them as they went down the stairs. Marielle followed a few paces behind them. Tamerlan couldn't see her and the spirits were too obsessed with him to notice her. Why him? Why did they all plague him? They didn't seem to notice Etienne or the Windsniffer and Liandari.

It was hard to watch the Harbingers working with Tamerlan. It ached to think that they could help while she was stuck. She just wanted to be with them. She just wanted to help with this fight – whatever it was. She clenched her fists, watching as the Legends grew more frenzied. They whirled around Tamerlan like dry leaves in the wind. Whispering, whispering, whispering.

And then she felt him.

"The Grandfather," she whispered and her eyes left Tamerlan as she searched for him.

He was here somewhere. She could feel it. She could locate almost anyone now that she was in the clock. She wasn't sure how, only that she could, like swimming in a current. You could guide where the current took you, but you couldn't control the current.

She smelled his foul insanity – the astringent scent of elderberry and malicious intent – rust-like and powerful. The insanity warped the colors around him, making them more vibrant but much less stable.

If she could just see how he flashed through time and space – maybe she could duplicate that, too. Maybe, she wouldn't have to stay in this clock …

26: BENEATH THE EMBALMERS' GUILD

TAMERLAN

A large *crack* split the air and a cry. He jumped the last four steps, landing in a crouch to see Liandari in a heap on the ground in front of him, her sword still clattering over the stone. Etienne stood in front of him, blade raised, coat swirling around him.

They'd been right.

The Grandfather was here.

The Grandfather rushed toward them in the green glow of the light on this lower floor, his hands held out. He was in front of them but then suddenly he was behind Etienne with his hands wrapped around the man's throat as if there had been no distance at all between one point and the next.

Tamerlan bit back a curse, but he needed no more prodding. Desperately, he jammed the rolled paper in his mouth, pulling on it like a dying man sucking in his last breaths.

His mind cleared and he was rushing forward, tube of paper still stuck to his lower lip, as the Legend took his body.

Maid Chaos.

Dragon's spit! Fear and rage shot through him and for a moment he wasn't sure if it was his fear and rage over having drawn her from the Legends or hers over the Grandfather's presence in her shrine.

Use the Eye!

She leapt at the Grandfather like a jungle cat leaping out on its prey. Glee filled her mental voice as she ripped him off Etienne's back by sheer force, lifting him in Tamerlan's arms and flinging him against the stone wall beside them. There was a cracking sound.

He should have slumped to the ground, but Legends didn't slump. He was back on his feet in an instant, dodging back behind the glowing thing at the center of the room.

Tamerlan finally caught a good look at it and if he'd been in charge of his body, he would have frozen in horror. He was not. Maid Chaos laughed with his voice, delight filling her at the grisly sight.

Whoever had done that to a once-living thing either had taken great care out of respect or out of a grisly obsession.

Standing rigid and half-wrapped stood a black, shriveled … thing. That it had once been human was – possible – though not clear. What flesh it once had was dried and clung to the bones like peel to fruit. Whether it was male or female was beyond telling. Someone had wrapped it from feet to waist in woven cloths. But from the waist up, the cloths were torn, stained, and jagged – as if the creature had enough life to pull them off that far but no farther. It glowed a sickly green. Why did it glow? That made no sense at all.

Floating around the ancient remains were glowing glass jars filled with piles of dust and the dust glowed green and seemed to writhe within the sealed jars.

My avatar.

He'd thought that Maid Chaos was a beautiful woman with flowing blonde hair and a breastplate of gold.

I was. In life.

But the other avatars had been recognizable. Deathless Pirate had clearly been himself. Queen Mer had been like her legends. The Grandfather had been untouched by the ravages of time.

My people tried their best. Their efforts were not perfect. They wanted to maintain life in my corporal body long past the time. It was a valiant attempt.

And a horrific result.

I bathe in horror. I revel in desecration.

And she was in his mind. Controlling his body. His soul shuddered.

And she wasn't staying still.

As the Grandfather dashed behind her avatar, banging and clanging as he reached for some implement off a nearby rack, Maid Chaos followed. She drew Tamerlan's sword letting it drag along the scabbard, so it came out with a rasping sound as she laughed.

Not the sword! The Eye.

I'm going to kill him. I don't need an Eye for that!

"As it was written long ago, '*She will dash him to the rocks. She will defy time. She will say – no further!*' My followers used that prophecy to guide them in the creation of this avatar, but today it comes true in your presence, Grandfather. Today, I slay you."

She leapt forward, but he was faster. He stepped out from the rack of tools with a large sickle – the type used to collect spices for embalming. But this one was larger than any Tamerlan had ever seen. What would you cut with that? It was nearly the size of a scythe.

"So easily you misinterpret. As always, Clarissa. You could never see past the moment," the Grandfather said. And with a single sweep of his scythe, he slashed through the avatar, cutting her clean through at the waist and smashing the floating jars.

The lights went out.

But Maid Chaos' scream through Tamerlan's throat seemed to go on forever. It echoed through time and space until it seemed like Tamerlan might have a living scream within him for the rest of his life.

27: Chaos Incarnate

Marielle

How was Anglarok not smelling this? All Marielle could smell was Legend – at first, she'd thought the scent was madness she knew now what it was – it was Legend. The smell of madness distilled over hundreds of years and made more potent, more powerful. It leaked all around Tamerlan like the drain of an alley leaking out to the canal, mixing in and out of his golden scent like a woven basket.

Maid Chaos had him completely in her grasp and to Marielle's eyes, her ghostly shape was overlaid over Tamerlan's normal human shape. His actions seemed delayed a half-second after hers – as if she were controlling them. And wasn't that because she was?

That was his secret. His horrible, deadly secret.

Realization flooded over her, leaving her chilled. In Jingen, when the Butcher of the Temple District had strode through the streets slaying anyone in his path it really had been

Tamerlan. And it really had been Maid Chaos. Suddenly – Marielle was seeing everything clearly.

When he'd given an eye to stop the dragon that really had been King Abelmeyer. And it had really been Tamerlan.

He was everything she knew him to be – a heroic, compassionate, intelligent man. And everything she feared – horrific, deadly, and murderous. He was both what she'd feared and what she'd hoped all wrapped into one. Who could have imagined such a thing?

A light flared and Marielle saw everything at once before it was suddenly extinguished again. Etienne holding the lantern over his head with a look of worried puzzlement on his face. Liandari slumped on the ground, eyes closed. Anglarok curled in on himself against the smell, moaning in pain. The avatar a ruined mess of ancient cloth, shattered glass, dust, and dried meat in a crude tangle on the floor. Tamerlan screaming, his face a mask of agony as he charged after the darting shape of the Grandfather.

The Grandfather snatched the lantern from Etienne as he passed, dashing it against the wall. A crash followed by darkness.

And then Marielle was hurrying to chase them. The light of the room above hit her like the blow of a hammer, but she had no physical body to deal with, no physical eyes to squint in pain.

The Grandfather rushed out onto the streets of Choan, Tamerlan at his heels. He was fast, but Tamerlan was faster. As they ran past the little fence surrounding the Embalmers, Maid

Chaos reached out and pulled a bar from the fence as easily as if it were a twig from a bush.

"My last run will be one for the stories, Grandfather!" she yelled, hurling the bar at his back.

It bounced off and he stumbled out into a knot of men dressed like the nameless who had served Liandari and Anglarok. They attacked without warning, harpoons stabbing. The first in the group stabbed out at the Grandfather, but the Legend was too fast for him. He grabbed the harpoon, flicking it with so much power that the nameless who had attacked him spun through the air like a discarded rag. Two more leapt toward the Grandfather but the harpoon he'd stolen spun in his hands, swiping each of them out of the way.

Tamerlan had caught up now. He leapt toward the Grandfather, his sword flashing in the light of morning.

Oranges, trampled to mush, filled the streets, coating everything in sticky juice and filling the world with the scent of citrus. But Marielle smelled more than oranges. She smelled terror – raw red swirls that burnt her nose with the smell of vinegar tangled between houses and guild buildings. She could smell the people within, hiding in terror, some hurt, some dead. She smelled their blood as it slicked the walls of the buildings and flowed through the streets. She shuddered at the thought of it.

Had they stepped into a battle?

The ground beneath them shook, making both the Grandfather and Tamerlan stumble as they engaged in a duel so fast that Marielle struggled to see every movement. Sword met harpoon, spun toward the head of the opponent, missed as he ducked, immediately lashed out at his feet, whistled through the air as he leapt, twisted to slash mid-body. The strokes grew faster, faster, faster as they pressed the attack. Maid Chaos versus Grandfather Timeless. It looked almost as if the two had sparred a thousand times before. As if they knew every move the other would make and were already countering it before the opponent could even move. But if the Grandfather won it wouldn't be Maid Chaos who died. It would be Tamerlan.

He had to win.

If he lost, all was lost.

And he would be lost, too. He needed saving as badly as she did – saving from the Legends.

Marielle snuck closer, closer, closer until she was at his back. Maid Chaos stepped back, dodging a blow, and just like that, Marielle was in Tamerlan's mind with him, looking through his eyes, watching the gleam in the Grandfather's Eye as they pressed the attack.

She hadn't meant to do that.

Meant to do what?

That was his voice!

Marielle? Is that you?

Shut up, you two! I'm trying to concentrate. Maid Chaos's mental growl actually stung.

Marielle felt like her eyes should grow wide. This wasn't supposed to happen like this. She wasn't supposed to be inside his mind. But unlike Maid Chaos, she had no control over his actions. No control over what he might do – or not do. She felt his helplessness. Felt his desperation for the Legend to succeed and destroy Grandfather Timeless.

And the Maid could fight. She held her own, matching the Grandfather move for move. In Tamerlan's body, she might even be faster than him. The Grandfather spun to the side, avoiding a clump of Choan guards as they rushed into the enemy with battle cries. She followed him, dodging the nameless who rushed to counter the guard. None of them seemed to care about the two Legends with the private duel, but indifferent blades could kill just as quickly. And they were fighting their duel in the middle of an invasion.

The Grandfather spun suddenly to the side, leaping up onto the top of an orange seller's cart. The seller was long gone, hiding, fighting, or dead. But the oranges fell in every direction from the over-full cart as the Grandfather scrambled over them. Maid Chaos leapt after him, scrambling over falling oranges and fighting for speed as she had to scramble for footing, too. The Grandfather climbed from the cart to an awning, his feet slipping over the angled cloth as he fought for purchase. Tamerlan reached after him, snagging the back of his coat and tugging hard.

It worked. The Grandfather stumbled backward, hands clawing for purchase, but there was nothing to grab. His harpoon spun away and he fell backward into the cart, leaping back to his feet and running down the street, oranges rolling after him.

Tamerlan followed, climbing up to the tiled rooftops, shoving his sword in the scabbard and then half-running, half climbing up one peak, only to half-run, half-slide down the other side.

One more roof and they'd be at the canal, but Maid Chaos showed no signs of stopping.

Destroyed. Destitute. Torn from the land of Legends! He will pay for what he did to me!

She pushed all her fury into Tamerlan's legs, flying over the rooftops as she watched her prey running on the ground. She didn't notice or care when she hit the angle wrong and twisted his ankle. Didn't pause as she left scraped skin and flecks of blood over the roof tile.

The Grandfather was fiddling with something. Was that a scrap of the bandages that had been around her avatar? What was he doing with those?

A trophy! He took a trophy?

Fury bled through her mind and then she was speeding up again. How could she be running faster?

Marielle felt like she was holding her breath – an unwilling passenger on the world's most terrifying ride. Why did Tamerlan allow this? Why did he invite it? It was horrifying. It stole her humanity away – her agency.

They flew through the air as Maid Chaos leapt from the final roof, her legs treading air as she tried to keep her balance as she fell.

Below them, the Grandfather had just scrambled into a gondola. He argued with the gondolier, making demands.

They were going to miss the gondola by inches. Marielle could see it. Maid Chaos twisted slightly in the air and out of the corner of Tamerlan's eye, Marielle saw the gondolier make eye contact with them. Jhinn! He stuck his oar in the water and heaved, sending the bow just under the falling Tamerlan.

"Ooof!" The sound was torn from Tamerlan's lungs as he hit the hull of the boat, landing in a crouch.

But Marielle's attention was on something else. The Grandfather swirled, spiraling around so fast it was like he was a child's top spinning. Yellow and purple sparks flicked all around him, popping and crackling and then he was gone.

But she'd seen it happen.

And she was relatively certain that she could do it, too.

Maybe.

Under the right circumstances.

The ground heaved under them, rocking the gondola. Out of the corner of Tamerlan's eye, she saw the Grandfather getting up out of a crouch in the street up above the canal. He was grinning as he looked down at the gondola.

Tamerlan, she started to say, but just like that – like the closing of a door in her face – something slammed between them and she was out of his mind and body.

The last thing she heard was a loud curse from Maid Chaos.

28: Come Back!

Tamerlan

Marielle? Marielle! Come back!

She'd disappeared as quickly as Maid Chaos had, leaving him shaking in the boat with his hands on his ringing ears.

Bring us back! Bring us back!

Open the Bridge!

Dragon. Dragon. Dragon.

The roar of their voices was overwhelming, making thought difficult. He gritted his teeth against the pain of it and braced himself as the gondola jolted. A huge wave rippled across the canal, carrying everything on its swell. Smoke rose in the distance as battles continued around the city.

"Smoke again! Smoke again!" It took him a moment to realize it was Jhinn screaming at him and not one of the Legends. He was pointing at the Grandfather from where he looked down on the canal laughing. "I saw Marielle and the golden-haired lady. You can smoke again and get them back!"

"She didn't use the Eye. I begged her to, but she didn't use it."

Jhinn didn't listen. He fumbled in the back of the boat, moving so quickly that when he pulled out the tiny wooden box with the paper rolls in it, some of them spilled across the gondola floor. Urgently, he scooped one up, lighting the end in his gondola lantern. He jammed it in Tamerlan's mouth.

She'd been there. Marielle. Jhinn had seen it, too! Tamerlan sucked in smoke like drinking water after a run, hoping to hear her voice. Hoping for the strength to catch the Legend again.

Yes! He could almost feel Lila's fist pounding the air as she snatched his body, winked at Jhinn and then leapt off the gondola to scale the smooth stone wall up to the street. She was as effortless in her motions as a spider crawling up a web. *Stick with me, pretty man and I will have you begging me to stay. You still have more of that mixture, right? Keep it around and we'll rule the world you and me!*

Lila? Why Lila and not Maid Chaos again?

She scaled the wall and flung herself over the railing. She was running almost before she leapt from it, skidding to a halt at the sight of the Grandfather battling Etienne, Liandari, and Anglarok all at once.

I didn't think you'd be sorry to feel her leave.

He hadn't been.

She's gone. Gone forever. When the Grandfather killed her, it destroyed her for all eternity. She only had as long as her spirit could hold on to you.

Swords and harpoon met the Grandfather's blade in a quick dance, but he was already spinning, purple and yellow sparks flying in every direction. He disappeared with a *pop*.

Tamerlan spun around looking for him along the rooftops and down the street, but he was nowhere to be seen. Wasn't Lila upset that he'd killed Maid Chaos? Wasn't she troubled by that?

Not particularly. I never liked her. I prefer to drink wine, not blood.

Then why complain that he'd killed her?

The chaining of magical creatures – particularly ones as big as dragons – is a complicated process requiring renewed magic.

Great, change the subject. His eyes were still studying every rooftop and alley he could see, looking for the Grandfather.

I'm not changing the subject. Renewed magic is part of the answer.

Etienne had told him about that. The mandala that the people walked through the city streets helped hold the dragon in place. So did the Lady Sacrifice's blood every year.

Fail on either count, and the dragon wakes.

"What just happened?" Anglarok asked, spinning like Tamerlan was. His scarf was wrapped so thick around his mouth that his words were muffled. "Have we lost him again?"

He avoided Tamerlan's eyes and Tamerlan wanted to blush at that. The man thought he was insane.

You are insane, or maybe you're the sanest of us all. Who knows? Lean into it. Your insanity is more powerful than their dull sanity.

The ground rumbled beneath their feet again.

"What is that?" Liandari asked, her face pale.

Etienne exchanged a look of understanding with Tamerlan. They'd both felt this before.

But Choan had sacrificed their Maid Chaos. Choan had people walking out the mandala on her streets. In fact, they were running the mandala right now, chasing and being chased all over the city as they fought the invaders.

There's a third thing that also must not fail – the initial binding.

Initial binding?

Every generation has to deal with dragons. The question is not whether they will rise, but what your generation will do when they come for you. Will your generation stand the test? Will anyone rise who can bind the dragon?

The initial binding? Was she suggesting that Maid Chaos had bound the dragon Choan? That somehow the destruction of her avatar nullified that binding?

Why else do you think Choan is rising?

He shivered under her control as the ground under them shivered again.

"Tamerlan! TAM!" Jhinn's voice was faint, but Tamerlan dashed to the railing and looked down at the boy. He pointed in the distance to where boats choked the canal, white boats filled with the Retribution.

They were bearing down the canal, lighting every boat they saw on fire.

Horror filled Tamerlan. Those weren't just trading boats and gondolas. Some were family boats. And most were operated by Waverunners who would die in the water or by the flames. He clenched his jaw. He didn't care what Lila wanted, they had to save Jhinn.

And avoid the dragon's wrath.

She could just keep her opinions to herself.

Did I say anything?

She launched him over the rail and took up a stance in the bow as she drew her sword.

She wasn't going to fight him on this?

Just you and me against an army? Sounds like fun. Maybe when we're done, we can find the Grandfather.

And just like that, he saw the old man, running along the rooftops heading in the opposite direction of the raging boats of the Retribution.

"That way!" he called to Jhinn. "We'll avoid the invaders and try to keep the Grandfather in our sights!"

Why didn't the Grandfather just leave the city?

There is something here that he wants, and I am determined that he should not get it.

Jhinn began to spin the boat around at the same moment that it jostled, shoving deeper into the water and rocking violently. Tamerlan spun to see Liandari, Anglarok, and Etienne recovering from their leap into the boat.

"Glad to see that you've joined us," Lila said with his voice. She sounded almost glib. "You're just in time. We have invaders chasing us, bent on our destruction, the dragon beneath the city is rising, and the Grandfather is outdistancing us. Oh, and if he gets to his goal before we do, he'll unleash destruction on these five cities unlike anything you've ever seen."

"We've seen dragons rise before," Etienne said quietly.

"But have you seen the Legends ride them?" Lila asked. "No? Then let's make sure that you never do."

29: UNTHINKABLE

MARIELLE

She'd seen it! She'd seen exactly how to pop in and out of time! And now she just needed to try it. But to try it, she'd need a body and hers was stuck in a clock.

If she'd had a body, she would have had to swallow down the acid rising in her throat. Because claiming a body could only mean one thing. There was only one person offering his body to spirits right now. And that was Tamerlan.

The fool!

The utter, incomprehensible fool. She wanted to throttle him. No cause was great enough to risk losing everything like that. He was risking his sanity, his humanity, his agency – everything!

Her thoughts stuttered to a stop. Really, Marielle? No cause? What about justice? Hadn't she sworn an oath that she would do anything necessary to preserve justice? Would she have risked her sanity for it? The sanity of others? The lives of others?

Where did you draw the line? When the choice wasn't between good and bad but between bad and worse. When the risks were uncertain and the outcomes opaque – where did you lay out a line and guard it like the wall of a palace?

She wished she knew.

But there was a clear answer somewhere. She just had to find it. And she had to try to find a way to do this without taking over his body. Because she would never be able to forgive herself if she violated someone else that way.

She searched, diving through time like a dolphin, searching, searching, searching for another way. A way that would keep them both from doing the unthinkable.

30: Bell Tower

Tamerlan

Whatever that device was that Jhinn had made to propel the gondola was worth ten times its weight in gold. Etienne worked the pedals, sweat beading on his forehead as a watchful Jhinn used his oar to steer the boat between the other escaping craft.

Lila had Tamerlan perched at the very front of the boat, holding the ferro and leaning over the dark brackish water as she kept his eyes on the Legend. She ignored the whispers between Anglarok and Liandari.

But Tamerlan was listening.

"We gave oath," Anglarok reminded her.

"Is the oath more important or the Retribution? It's started, Anglarok. There is glory to be won, a greater name, a new set of beaches on my skin!"

He snorted. "A woman is only worth what weight her word can bear. Stay the course."

Lila leapt so quickly that Tamerlan – distracted by their words – didn't have time to mentally brace himself. He heard the shouts of his companions from behind him, but she was already leaping from one boat to the next, ignoring their cries as she chased the Grandfather.

A squawking chicken flew up in front of him and she batted it to the side, leaping right over the head of an old Waverunner woman as she cursed at Tamerlan. Lila narrowly avoided a swinging oar as one gondolier took a swipe at him and then they were at the canal wall, Lila scaling it with lightning speed. She could find a handhold or foothold in rock so slick that Tamerlan would have thought it impossible to climb.

They emerged on the street, running through a clump of Choan guard.

"You there! Join the guard or consider yourself an enemy!"

By the time the guard got to 'enemy', he was already past, streaking up the wall of a nearby building – a trade consortium topped by a massive bell tower. He'd seen a tower like that before in Jingen.

The Trade House. It's a common feature. In there they set the price of goods for the city daily – wheat, flax, oranges, iron – if you can name it, they are selling and trading it in there. They ring the bell to announce changes in the exchange.

The Grandfather seemed set on reaching the bell. His wiry frame was already scaling the white stone tower, red scarf rippling in the morning breeze. Lila followed at an almost alarming speed, as if she'd been climbing bell towers her whole life.

I have been.

As if she had no fear scaling the slick wall.

I don't.

As if she really thought they could catch the Grandfather up there.

He works his head into the noose! Where can he flee to from the top of a tower? Will he sprout wings and flap away? Fool! He chose my stomping grounds – the world above, the world of thieves and rogues.

And this time she would use the Eye, right? She'd make sure he was bound so they could get himt o the clock.

Haven't you realized yet that we aren't going to use your precious Eye?

We?

The Legends.

But Abelmeyer used it on the dragon!

You're our one link to this world. What good are you to us blind?

But she had promised!

I lie to you. Often. Don't let it sour your mood.

The city below them looked like the tide rushing over a beach. The ground still shook with rolling tremors, but from the sea, a wave of white washed over the city – the sails and banners of the Retribution were all white gilded with golden edges.

Chaos is when I thrive. People don't notice a trifle gone in the middle of a war.

How had she become a Legend? He couldn't imagine her doing anything selfless or noble. She'd already admitted to being a liar.

She snorted. *And you thought Maid Chaos could be noble? Clearly, you didn't understand the depths of her cruelty. Or the Grandfather – do you think him selfless? We all do things for our own reasons. Sometimes, a selfish person might do something that seems selfless to achieve their selfish end. A madwoman might do something seemingly noble for reasons so insane they can't be delved. Don't think you can judge by actions. You only ever see a small piece.*

Who would have thought that a thief would lecture him on morality?

Do you want to catch the Legend or don't you?

His arms burned from the effort of climbing. Lila glanced down briefly and his head swam at how much higher they were than the gondola they'd left below. Jhinn was staring up at them, hand shielding his eyes. Hopefully, he got over that and kept fleeing. That fleet wasn't going to stop just because Tamerlan had.

This tower was so high that he was surprised he hadn't noticed it before they started climbing.

You were preoccupied.

And they were almost at the top. How was the Grandfather going to ride a dragon from up here? It made no sense.

He's off course. I drove him up here.

The Grandfather flung himself over the lip of the small wall surrounding the bell and Tamerlan was just a few spans beneath the lip. They'd gained a lot of ground.

I am the greatest climber who ever lived. The greatest schemer. The most triumphant of all. See why you should give yourself to me? Let me guide you down a fresh path – a path to prosperity.

He wasn't even sure if survival was an option for him. Never mind prosperity. And both those things came far below redemption. He just wanted to get right again, somehow.

Sure. We can do that, too.

They flipped over the edge of the wall into the bell tower like a fish over the side of a boat, landing in an artful crouch. Tamerlan's knife was in his hand before he'd stuck the landing.

"And who is possessing you today?" the Grandfather asked from where he leaned against the massive brass bell. His reflection was warped and twisted in the bell – just like the Legend being reflected. "Maid Chaos is gone. I'd like to know whose avatar to target next."

"You'll never find it," Lila laughed in Tamerlan's voice. "It's not revered like yours is. There aren't religions built on me."

"Ram the Hunter?" the Grandfather asked, and Lila laughed again.

"Hardly."

"I was Time for a while – still have some of those tricks up my sleeves." He shot his cuffs dramatically and sparks leapt out from them. "I can find out where anyone's avatar was put. All I have to do is to go and look."

Lila laughed again. "Well, that assumes you're free to look. And for once, I want what the kid wants. I want you back in that clock."

The Grandfather's smile looked more like a death rictus.

"Then catch me – if you can."

He shoved the bell, hard. It barely moved, though a small gong sound – as if the clapper had barely brushed the massive bell – filled the air.

Leaping onto the lip of the small wall around the bell, he leaned out over the city below like a bird about to catch flight. As he spread his arms, Lila was already dashing forward. As he lifted his face into the sun, she was leaping toward him.

What was she thinking? She was going to kill them! His heart was in his throat, racing so fast that his vision was blacking in and out.

The Grandfather dove from the tower, leaping up and then somersaulting to leap headfirst in his dive. Lila tumbled after him – less graceful, more flailing arms and legs than an actual dive.

Tamerlan screamed inside. Fear and panic flooding through him like water through a canal. He was going to die! What had she done?

Bright purple and gold sparks danced around the Grandfather and he began to whirl in midair. He was about to pop out of this time and place and into another – again. He had the luxury of that.

Lila clenched the smoking roll of Spice between his teeth and the lit end flared brightly as the wind sped around it.

Smoke it! Let me stay!

He had no chance of getting free of her – not like that!

Get free and you will die. I'm your only hope.

Beneath them, the city rose up like a living map about to swallow them up.

He sucked in the smoke.

He felt a sudden push.

Oh. This is a surprise.

31: Yellow and Purple Sparks

Marielle

She had Tamerlan in her clutches, the weasel! She'd tossed her red hair and laughed just before she grabbed him and threw him at the Grandfather back along the canal and she was laughing still. Laughing as she drove him to his death. She smelled of careless certainty. The minty smell of that certainty was so strong that it almost overwhelmed the elderberry of her insanity. And the glint in her eye as she rode him down changed everything.

It was still wrong to take over someone else's mind. It was still wrong to let them do that to themselves. It was maybe even evil.

But sometimes you had to do something unthinkable to save someone. And Tamerlan needed saving as badly as she did.

Marielle blinked as she popped into space beside Lila where she clung to Tamerlan's back. Surprise was her only advantage. Before the Legend could notice her, she pushed with all her might, grabbing Tamerlan with her ghostly arms from behind, sinking her face into his shoulder. They had to be quick. They couldn't lose their one chance!

She had him! What a heady feeling! His mind and body were suddenly as much hers as her own ever had been. She could feel the beat of his heart in her chest, the breath of his lungs in her mouth. His golden scent – hot honey and cinnamon flooded her like the warmth of sunshine. But there was no time to bask.

She pulled his arms back and pulled his feet together so that he flew through the air more swiftly, angling toward the spinning Grandfather. His limbs were powerful as they moved, the ease of his movement a joy.

Focus, Marielle!

If she timed it just right …

Marielle? Dragon's Spit! Are you in my mind?

Yes.

She shuddered at the admission, flinching from how it stained her.

Don't leave. Please don't leave!

He sounded so desperate. Lonely.

Don't let me die alone – or worse – don't let me die with all of them fighting for me like scrabbling dogs.

Marielle reached for the Grandfather, physically and mentally. Loud sounds like cracks and pops of a fire filled her mind and then their vision was nothing but purple and yellow sparks as they were sucked into the whirl of the Grandfather.

She emerged on a butte overlooking a wide plain. The scents of it filled Marielle's nose – no wait, that was Tamerlan's nose. And they weren't her usual scent abilities. They were just regular smells – the smells of grass and fragrant bushes. She felt blind for a moment with this dull nose until she saw the colors.

They made no sense! They weren't full of scent. They were just there – everywhere. Not swirling or trailing or glowing, just there as if each object had its own. And they were vibrant and full and distracting. They were so stunning that it took her a moment to realize that the Grandfather was creeping along the edge of the butte looking down.

He's going to see me.

But he was wrong about that. Marielle could still smell the Grandfather's emotions – sort of. It was like trying to smell through a thick scarf, but it was still there if she fought for it. What she smelled most was interest and excitement swirling around him in wide bands. He was watching something.

Tamerlan? Are you okay in there? I'm sorry that I stole your body. I just didn't want you to die.

Dragon's spit, Marielle! Do you think I'm angry about that? I'm relieved. I'm glad that you're okay – that we both still live!

Marielle crept Tamerlan closer, careful not to make a sound. They needed to get the Grandfather. Now. Before he leapt again. And she didn't dare leave Tamerlan yet. What if the Grandfather leapt and Tamerlan couldn't chase after him?

He pulled a deep breath through the tube of Spice in his lips. Strange that he could choose to do that when she had control of every other aspect of him. It tasted almost good. Like smoke, sure, but fragrant and almost tasty. She breathed it in like life. The longer he had it in him, the longer she'd stay to help.

Don't go, Marielle.

He felt so familiar. His body felt like home. And yet it was nothing like hers. Large where hers was small. Narrow where hers was wide. Wide where hers was narrow. It gave her a giddy feeling of being totally at home in a foreign place.

She just had to be sure that no one else could shove her away the way she'd shoved Lila. She could still see them there, floating around her – the Legends. They wanted Tamerlan back. They lurked just over the Bridge, biding their time, waiting for their chance, with wicked, gleaming red eyes.

Didn't he see that when he called them? Didn't he see that they wanted him, not to help him, but to own him like a slave, like a shared avatar used to give them second life?

She could see it plainly. The Grandfather was a problem for the Dragonblood Plains. But these Legends were just as dangerous. They were consuming her friend's soul.

Do you see what he's looking at?

She wasn't looking at that. She was trying to maneuver silently behind him. If she could hit him over the head with something, or stab him with the knife Tamerlan still held …

Did he need to be alive to replace her in the clock? She wasn't a murderer, but this might classify as self-defense.

It's the Smudgers! They fled from the five cities to somewhere north and west. This is them! Look at their burning braziers!

Knowing that didn't help them to catch the Grandfather. And that was her only goal.

They all went somewhere and no one knew where or how, but do you see what they're doing? They have that woman lifted up on a platform, pinned spread eagle over it in the sun. That must be awful. She's probably going mad from the heat. Are they passing smoking braziers under her?

She needs to be rescued.

She took a careful step toward the Grandfather, easing her weight onto the balls of her feet and then lifted the other foot. It was harder to maneuver Tamerlan's body. She wasn't used to such long legs or to so much weight in the shoulders.

Look! Something's happening! Look!

But she was trying not to look. One more step and she'd be on him.

"Dragon's spit and the entrails of the Legends!" The Grandfather's vulgarity spilled out like a cup knocked over. "They've made her again."

Now was the time! While he was distracted!

Wait! Do you see it? She's tearing the ropes up! She's ripping the bracing from the platform. She's leaping down!

Marielle sprang forward, stabbing toward the Grandfather, but he twisted away as if he could see her lunge behind his back. He spun, caught her gaze, spat a curse, and then the purple and yellow sparks erupted.

Marielle leapt forward, catching his coat with a hand as he whipped through time and space.

Did you see that? Didn't you see that? Tamerlan was babbling. *I think they put a spirit into her with all that smoke. I think – is it crazy that I think they put Maid Chaos into her? That she might be Maid Chaos reborn?*

What was crazy was that he was so obsessed with it. What mattered right now was the Grandfather. What mattered was putting him back in the clock. They could deal with any violations of the law that the Smudgers had made later when both of them were whole and free of Legends.

The law never rested. It never slept. It would come for those Smudgers with slow, trudging steps.

But this will never end, Marielle. Not if we don't stop it at the source.

What did he mean by 'we'? Since when was it their job to stop all evil? It was her job to enforce the law. Both the laws of the cities and the real law. But the fates of Legends and worlds were not hers to be responsible for. As if she wasn't already burdened enough!

That's fine, Marielle. You don't need to take this on. You've done enough.

His words were compassionate, and yet they stung. He made it sound like she wasn't sufficient. Like she'd settled for something less than his great cause.

No, no, not at all. It's just that all this is my fault. And I have to find some way back into humanity. Some way out of the madness. Some way to heal all the wounds I've gouged, rebuild all the buildings I've crumbled, wash away the tears I caused.

The way he said that – like he was drowning, like he just wanted air for a moment …

The only way to do that is to find evil at its core and destroy it. The only way is to break the chains our people have been put under and finally set them free.

What did that have to do with the Smudgers? What did that have to do with the Legends?

I don't know yet. I just know that I have to keep diving deeper until I find the source.

The whirling stopped and they fell back into time.

32: Triumph of the Mother

Marielle

The Grandfather was hard to catch. She couldn't blame Tamerlan for taking so long to catch up with him when the Grandfather slipped through her own fingers so fast that she could barely gasp and he was gone. And Tamerlan's body didn't work like hers, didn't run like hers, or jump like hers. What made it worse was that she didn't want to have to think about the fact that she was currently possessing him. It was – a violation of sorts.

Your mind is nice inside mine. Like a pool of fresh water. Cool. Transparent. Easy.

It didn't help that his thoughts caressed her mind, swirling gently around it, seeming to be everywhere at once like an embrace.

She tried to force away mindfulness of that kind of intimacy and focus on the work at hand. They had a Legend to catch. And if she let Tamerlan go right now one of the other Legends would grab him and do whatever they wanted with him – and that wouldn't mean catching Grandfather Timeless.

He was on the rooftops. She could smell him if she focused. He smelled of insanity – the elderberry scent astringent even in her weakened ability to smell – and of the charcoal mists of time that puffed to cloud the memory. She focused on that smell, letting her mind name it and remember it so that she could follow it anywhere. And then she opened Tamerlan's eyes.

They were balanced on a rooftop.

She'd thought at first that it was Choan, but the white waves of the invaders were not present. The tang of the brackish sea was not there. No … this was another city of the Dragonblood Plains. Beneath her, in the streets, the Orange Wars were waging as people tossed oranges at one another and engaged in mock skirmishes. There was some laughter. Some scuffling with minor injuries. Marielle had never liked Autumngale. The scent of competition and brotherhood swirling through the air in carrot orange and the smell of apple cider was nice, but the complicated swirls of musky green envy and the puffs of russet ambition irritated her nose.

And this Autumngale, there was something more.

She wrinkled Tamerlan's nose, trying to catch it.

I hate to sound impatient, but do you think we should be chasing him?

Yes. Of course. He pulled another lungful of smoke from the roll of Spice balanced on his lips – asking for her to stay. The burning end was almost gone.

Light another one. They're in my inner pocket.

She fumbled inside and found the oilcloth roll, carefully extracting one before wrapping the others. Urgency bit at her, but if she wasn't careful, and she ruined these rolls, this might be the end of their chance. Carefully, she lit one with the other, replacing the old stub for a new roll between Tamerlan's lips.

Okay. Now, to run.

She took off across the rooftops, combining Tamerlan's greater strength and larger muscles with her own street experience to push him harder and faster across the rooftops than she had ever been able to go.

And more skillfully than I could.

She ignored the compliment, focusing – searching with her nose.

This way!

She followed the trail up a tile roof, using Tamerlan's feet to climb the slippery tiles. The Grandfather wasn't far ahead.

Below, a roar ripped through the crowd and she glanced down to see a cloud of orange – oranges flying through the air and in the streets and on the wall and the carrot orange smell of sport puffing around them. That was fine. Just the Autumngale celebration.

Her grip slipped and she fell slightly, catching herself in time, but the knife in Tamerlan's right hand skimmed across his leg leaving a gouge.

Oh no.

Calm. It will be okay.

I cut you!

She shook, at the thought. She'd taken someone's body and cut them with their own knife.

An accident.

But taking him hadn't been an accident.

I welcomed you.

Not good enough. She clenched his jaw, sheathed the blade and stood still, glued in place while her breathing grew more and more rapid.

Can I have just a little control over my body?

Oh, dragon's spit! Why hadn't she … fumbling mentally, she tried to find a way to give it to him without surrendering to the triumphant looking spirits around them. Their fingers seemed longer as they reached for him. She felt his mind grow stronger, gently nudging her aside. The touch was close – as close as a brush cheek to cheek would be.

There we go. Let's calm down a little. Deeper breaths. Yes, there you go.

It was his body. So, why did it feel like he was taking care of *her?* He caressed her mind.

Easy now, easy. Let it out. Big breaths. You're going to be okay.

He said that like he'd said it a thousand times before.

I have. I tell myself that a lot. When life is too much. When I feel trapped. He paused. *You're going to be okay.*

She was going to be okay.

Let's follow the Grandfather. This is Yan and I think he's heading for the Palace.

She thought so, too. But why?

He was there before to get a book. Maybe he needs another book.

That seemed reasonable. She pulled in a long breath and then began to scramble again, ignoring the ache in her – his – leg where the knife had scored it.

Tamerlan?

Right here.

It felt almost as if his consciousness were holding hers – like the clasp of hands.

I'm sorry. I shouldn't have taken you over.

You did what was necessary. And I am grateful.

His mental voice felt warm on her consciousness,

They were climbing quickly now. Climb up one side of the roof, slide down the other. Jump to the next. But what would they do when they reached the first canal or a similar barrier that they couldn't cross?

Almost before she thought it, they were there. She stopped with a skid on the edge of the tile roof, a single tile falling from her quick stop and plunging over the edge of the roof into the street below.

She stared down. Had she hurt someone? Calls and cries drifted up and around the tile, a swell of red rolled over the street. But she didn't see anyone hurt and lying in the street. She could smell it now, though, the overpowering smell of violence – red and smoky.

Look.

She followed his mental prodding, looking toward where the crowds fought, and oranges flew through the air. But that wasn't all. Red swirled up and spattered outward, the scents mixing with actual colors. Someone was shedding blood.

"Variena!" someone in the crowd called. "Our savior! For Variena!"

That was her mother's name.

Just the thought of it sent a spike of sadness through her chest. She would probably never see her mother again. Like almost everyone else, she had probably perished when Tamerlan saved Marielle in Jingen and woke the dragon.

I am guilty of many things, but not the death of your mother.

She hadn't meant to accuse him. It just hurt to think of her, that was all.

I saw her alive and well in the refugee camps here just days ago. She looks like you.

Marielle felt like she'd frozen. He'd seen her?

Except she has brown eyes.

That was her!

Icy excitement filled her at the thought.

"Variena!" the cry was louder now and before Marielle's eyes, they surged into the streets – thin men and women with gaunt faces and wild eyes, swirling with the red smoky scent of violent determination. They came in a mass, their jaws set, and weapons held out. Where they met the groups of people throwing oranges, they waded in like harvesters to the wheat, hacking, chopping, stabbing. Not a change of expression filled their faces. Not a hint of sympathy. They came to conquer. And they came in the name of her mother.

She shivered, feeling suddenly cold to the core.

Do you see why I must end it all? I must find the root of all this trouble? Everything is wrong. Everything!

And then a new group plowed out onto the street. Yan Palace Guards in blue and gold tabards, holding their halberds high, marched like toy soldiers through the streets. They were minutes from clashing with the hollow-eyed uprisers. Moments and then they'd really see battle.

She held his breath in horrified anticipation. But when the groups met, they merged like two rivers, one clear and one muddy. They didn't intermingle, but they flowed side by side and while the uprisers screamed her mother's name, the guards chanted something else.

"For Variena and Decebal!"

"Decebal Zi'fen!"

"House Zi'fen!"

She felt like her eyes might dry out they'd gone so wide. She couldn't close them in her shock. Tamerlan's mind reached around hers, taking back control, pulling her back from the edge.

Both our families have brought disaster on this city.

She'd missed so much when she was in the clock. None of this seemed to be a surprise to him.

It is and it isn't all at the same time. Etienne warned me. I just wasn't listening.

She and Tamerlan had to fix it. She could see that. That's what he was going on about – fixing gouges and repairing wounds.

She sank into his mind like into a comforting hug as he slid down from the roof to a balcony and into the street, still racing toward the palace. They could do this if they worked together. She might have lost her sense of everything else, but that was the one thing she was certain was true.

33: All is Ever Lost

Tamerlan

Warmth and tenderness filled him. If he could preserve her from this hell, he would. Anything she needed. Any solace. Any help.

He was the only one who should go mad for this.

She was already plunging him through the crowds toward the palace, weaving between guards and revolutionaries. One of the Yan guards grabbed Tamerlan by the front of his shirt.

"Whose side are you," he began with a growl, but his words cut off as he glimpsed Tamerlan's face. "You look like him."

"I am Tamerlan Zi'Fen," Marielle said with his lips. It felt strange how she said his name – gently, like she was worried about breaking it.

The guard dropped him like a hot coal. "My apologies."

As they filed past, the other guards all shot him worried looks – earned, no doubt, by his father's behavior – but he was soon past them, as Marielle hurried through the streets and tried not to slip on the sticky peels and ruined fruit all over the ground. Any other Autumngale the feasting would start soon and the old rivalries would melt into one big feast and dance. Any other Autumngale, he'd have the day off to spend with friends.

But not today.

Today they hunted.

Marielle chased through the streets, skidding around a group of revolutionaries. Something big was going on by the palace. The crowds thickened as they approached it, but there was no fighting here. It was almost as if the fight had almost been won.

So easily?

So quickly?

That troubled him. Even as Marielle directed his body into the thick of things, he was watching. The signs of his father were here. Only Decebal would turn a population from their rulers after marrying one of his children into the ruling family.

Marielle was focused on the scent of the Grandfather. She was sniffing the air with his nose. But he was watching the crowd. Watching their faces as they drew closer to a crude platform still being constructed and a knot of somewhat better-armed refugees. Had he seen these faces before? They looked familiar.

They leapt forward as Marielle followed the scent, so obsessed that she didn't seem to realize they were headed right into the knot of the revolution's leaders. She was excited, like a dog hot on the trail.

He's close. He's close.

She needed to pull back. They were too close to the ringleaders. One of them was already snarling at him, pointing to him with a leather-gloved finger.

In front of them, another moved to shield a woman in a heavy cloak with her back to them. His arm whipped up, stopping Tamerlan at the same moment that the woman whirled to face them, the hood falling to reveal her face.

Variena.

Shock reverberated through Marielle. She must not have believed it, not really, not until now. The blood seemed to drain from his face at her reaction.

"You. The one who brought food," Variena said, looking at him with calculating eyes. "You seem to always arrive at just the right moment." Her smile was predatory. "Timeliness is a welcome trait in a man."

He tried to clench his jaw as he pulled in a puff of smoke from the roll of paper still hanging from his lips. Marielle was frozen with shock, like she'd been hit by a pole between the eyes.

Let me take over, Marielle. He pulled at her grip on him, sliding it from her mental hold.

"I'm afraid not," he said smoothly. "My appointment today is elsewhere."

"If you think to foul this up – you and that worthless piece of ruler scum – "

He hadn't realized she knew about Etienne but he was smooth in his interjection. "This has nothing to do with you. Not yet.

I'm just trying to prevent what happened in Jingen from happening here."

She leaned in close so that he could smell her clove-scented breath. "What happened in Jingen worked out just fine for me, pretty boy."

"But now you're on top," he said smoothly despite the sweat forming on his brow. She was a formidable woman. She had all of Marielle's assurance and none of her morality. "And those on top have the most to lose when the tables are flipped."

She grunted. "Don't get in the way or I'll carve that pretty face to ribbons."

Tamerlan gave her a crooked smile and pushed away, hurrying out of the crowd. Marielle – inside his mind – was upset. He felt her emotions ricocheting from one to the next as he drove them toward the palace. How was he going to get in there without her abilities to guide him? Could he use the same technique he'd used when Lila was guiding him? That seemed unlikely.

Just give me a moment to catch my breath.

He didn't have to worry. The bridge stretching across the canal to the palace doors was busy – but unguarded, the doors flung wide open.

Be careful. All is not as it seems.

This was worse than he'd thought. No one guarding the Palace? Had that ever happened before?

He picked up the pace, trotting up the bridge and dodging tattered refugees as they intermixed with Landholds. None of the Landholds looked happy. Their eyes kept flicking toward the Yan Palace Guard. And the Guard was everywhere. They weren't preventing movement and they weren't stopping anyone. One of the guards in a rumpled uniform lounged idly at the highest point of the bridge, looking leisurely over the people moving in and out of the palace. He seemed to be at his ease until his eyes squinted and his hands flicked out, grabbing a whey-faced Landhold from the bridge and hauling him over the rail and into the water with a single burst of energy.

There had been no warning. When he was done, he returned to seemingly lounging along the bridge. No one was fooled. The crowd moved like a group of rats surrounded by large cats.

The guards smell of madness.

But so did Tamerlan, according to Anglarok.

No one helped the gurgling Landhold from his place in the moat. The walls of the moat were slick and steep. His only hope would be to find a passing boat or to be a very strong swimmer.

Tamerlan swallowed, hurrying through the door with the rest of the crowd. It was hard to move quickly through the press of bodies.

He's just ahead! I can smell him! He's close!

He almost thought he could see what she meant, like a swirl of colored smoke up ahead. The more he focused on it, the harder it was to see. Perhaps, it was only his imagination.

He saw the scarf first – the red scarf waving in the wind. Like a dog with a fresh scent in his nose, it gave him a new burst of energy. He put his head down and ran, thrusting every ounce of power he had into long, powerful strides.

He was gaining. He could tell. He pushed past a screaming maid in the door of the palace, dodging the white linens she threw in his face in her terror. He was the least of her problems. He'd be gone before she could blink. She should be more worried about the guards on the bridge.

The Grandfather was only strides ahead as they raced up a shallow flight of stone stairs and then down a tapestry lined hall. Screams and cries of surprise rang out down the hall where the Grandfather ran ahead of him as Palace servants rushed away from the commotion. Tamerlan dodged past a wide-eyed man dressed like a butler – his hands full of silver candlesticks – and then as he ran into a pack of maids on their hands and knees scrambling for the dropped cutlery, he placed a hand on one of their shoulders and vaulted right over their bent heads. No time for civility. A woman dressed like a Landhold stood before him with her hands over her mouth, surrounded by shards of broken vases and a mirror that used to line the hall beside where she stood. He sprang past her without a second look.

The Grandfather cared nothing for the health or property of anyone. Like Time the ever-rolling stream, he carried all those things away – eventually.

The Library doors were wide open when Tamerlan finally skidded around the corner to them, panting and heaving with exertion. She was there again. Amaryllis.

His eyes caught on his sister standing with her back against the door. Caught the slight shake of her head. She didn't want acknowledgment. Or she didn't want him there. And either way, it stung.

Isn't that Amaryllis? The one you meant to save when you saved me instead?

Yes. No time for that.

He burst through the door.

I feel the great sadness in your heart at the sight of her.

She was well and she had a future. Asking for anything else was just selfishness.

And isn't love selfish sometimes? Doesn't it want to know that the beloved loves, too?

Not real love. Real love wanted what was best for the other no matter what the beloved thought of the lover.

What a cold approach. It doesn't sound like you at all.

He didn't want to think about it.

Because it stings.

And he didn't have to.

There was the Grandfather! He was grabbing a book off the shelf.

Tamerlan leapt, flying through the air arms reaching out. He knew without having to say anything – the Grandfather was about to jump through time and space again. The old man was already whirling, sparks pouring off him like water from a falls. His eyes met Tamerlan's as Tamerlan fell short, hitting the stone floor of the library with an *oof* as the breath was knocked out of him.

"You fell short," the Grandfather laughed. "In the end they all do!"

And then he vanished with a *pop*.

34: Whisper of Rebellion

Marielle

The pain bit at her. He held so much pain inside. So much rejection and hurt. When he thought he was hiding it, it oozed out of him like sap from a tree. No wonder he wanted so badly to save everything. No wonder he took refuge in the smoke with all that hurt building inside like thunderheads. He'd been such a beautiful boy with a sweet, artist's heart. She'd seen that again and again in the past.

But it was the fragility of his very sweetness, it was the vulnerability of his compassion that made it possible to shatter him. And he was shattered. She felt it as he tried to bury his pain at his sister's lack of acknowledgment. She felt it as he stuffed his loneliness past the shards of who he'd once been. Now, he was all loneliness and guilt in one rolled up murky ball.

Not *all*.

No, she was mistaken about that. Because even now as the Grandfather disappeared and he thought he'd lost him. Even now as frustration frizzled through him and he reached in his pocket and withdrew another roll of Spice – even now his thoughts were of her. His thoughts were of her in the clock and of the people of the Dragonblood Plains who would suffer because of him. Who would have expected such selflessness – such a sliver of sweet compassion under so much tangled bitterness, guilt and hurt?

She could smell it all woven through the honey and butter golden scent of him, twisting through like colored fibers in a golden rug.

She just wanted to hold him and let him cry until it had all leaked out of him in hot salty tears.

"Well, that's that then, isn't it?" he said aloud before taking a long pull on his fresh roll of spice.

Admit it, she prodded. You're disappointed.

"Devastated," he said aloud again. It was almost as if he were afraid to speak with his thoughts to her – as if he was shying away from the intimacy.

Can't you just let someone hold you and help you for a moment, Tamerlan? Can't you just cave in for a single second instead of carrying it all yourself?

"You don't understand," he said – aloud again in an empty library.

What didn't she understand?

If I give in, even for a moment, even for a fraction of a moment …

This time he spoke with his mind. And it *was* oddly intimate. Like the touch of two friends. Like the words of a long-time lover – so few, but so full.

…I'm afraid I'll break.

And what if he broke? Maybe that would be best?

Then who … He almost seemed to choke on the thought – as if it were too hard to think. As if just thinking it was already breaking him … *will put me back together?*

She reached with her mind for him. Reached the only way she knew how – in a way with no barriers and nothing denied. She reached with all her heart. She shouldn't. She already knew how dangerous it was to give all of yourself to anyone, never mind someone who was …

Insane? Hopelessly addicted? Guilty?

But she felt him taking her embrace, drawing all her mind and soul in like a puff of that smoke until she was swirling in his mind like it swirled in his lungs, until she didn't know where her longings ended and his started. Until she could touch where his heart was raw and his personality aching. Touch it with healing hands. Kiss it better – or at least try.

It was only the space of a single breath – and yet a world passed between them in that breath. He trembled under her touch – strong, powerfully strong, and yet so delicate in his pain. She couldn't heal it all – didn't try. She just sat with him in it.

I understand, she tried to tell him.

Understand what?

Understand everything.

And when he breathed out, she breathed out with him.

I've lost the Grandfather, he said eventually. *And that means that I can't get you out of the clock.*

Not quite, Marielle said. Do you still have my shell?

He pulled it from his belt pouch and she felt him smiling as he looked at it.

Would he mind if she took back control?

Before she could ask, he was letting go and the authority over his body returned to her. She lifted the shell to his lips and blew gently. She'd seen this in the ages upon ages in the clock and now she knew what it was – knew how a great of a gift she'd been given when Anglarok gave it to her.

It was a shell of echoes. Other shells might echo the sea but this one echoed magic. And she had the power to trigger it. She blew again and yellow and purple sparks began to rain down on them. Blew a third time, and they began to spin.

I had no idea it had such power.

It was just an echo. An echo of what had been here a moment before.

It was hard to let the moment in the library go. Hard to go back to the chase when there was still so much for them to settle.

If you don't, then you'll be stuck in the clock forever. Do you really want that?

Of course not. But she'd grown used to his mind. So used to it that she didn't want to leave.

Then don't. His invitation was a mental whisper, lifting every hair up along the back of her neck. *Stay with me.*

With a *pop,* they left the Library and with another, they landed in the square of the palace in Xin. Marielle recognized it immediately, and even if she hadn't she would have known where they were when she saw Allegra standing on the battlement addressing the crowd in just the same way that Lady Saga had only months ago when she'd been here with Etienne and the Harbingers.

She scanned the crowd for the Grandfather as Allegra's words boomed over the crowd.

"It is finished. The Whisper has taken Xin City."

Oranges formed a pulpy sludge beneath their feet and the people around them were streaked in sticky juice and blood, huddled in thick cloaks against the sea winds. Flies were already beginning to buzz, drinking in orange pulp and human blood with the same voraciousness. What a horrific celebration.

Here, too? Will any city be left?

Choan had fallen to the Retribution, Yan to Variena and Decebal, and Xin to the Whisper. That left only H'yi.

H'yi is a burnt-out hulk – barely a city at all.

Worry filled her, rising up like tidewaters. Were they ruined? Were they all ruined?

And then she caught sight of the Grandfather in the crowd, pushing through with a snarl on his face and a book in his hand. He seemed almost mad as he forced his way through the crowd. She took off running while Allegra's words followed her.

"We are your rulers now and we hereby declare an end to the nonsense that has ruled this city. There will be no more religions. The Smudgers are already gone. The Timekeepers are not welcome here. You will clear the Temple District immediately and it will be refurbished for industry. For long years, Xin city has been chained by superstition and ancient customs. Those end today."

A cheer burst from the crowd. Marielle barely managed to squeeze Tamerlan's body between the roaring people as they forced themselves forward, squeezing against the palace as if proximity alone could grant them a sliver of Allegra's power. But tattered clothing, blood-soaked bandages, and ruined fruit spoke a different story.

"There will be no more sacrifices. No more feast days. No more holidays that honor the Legends. If you see a shrine, a plaque, a statue, a tribute OF ANY KIND dedicated to a Legend, I order you to destroy it!" Allegra's words blazed across the wind that carried them through the square. "I am Allegra Spellspinner. I sell cures. And I am here to cure Xin!"

The roar of the people made her head ache.

I told Etienne she was a dangerous woman.

She was most certainly that. Marielle still wished she knew what her relationship to the former Lord Mythos was.

I think she wanted him to be her lover.

Unlikely. A woman like that cared for nothing but power.

Maybe she also cared about power over a man who once had been powerful.

That wasn't how Marielle thought. Who cared who had power or didn't? Power was only ever meant to be used for the good of humanity and the service of the law.

You are a rare pure gem in a well of snakes.

She felt his cheeks flushing at her emotion and quickly pushed it down. That was too weird.

There he was! Their quarry.

The Grandfather surfaced from the crowd again, pushing out toward the stairs that led down from the Government District to the districts below.

Marielle shoved through the crowd after him.

Careful! No need to hurt anyone!

Justice would be served. She was going to put the Grandfather back in the clock. If anyone deserved the sentence – it was him.

No need to trample anyone in the process!

She wasn't going to trample anyone. She was just going to catch him!

How long had Tamerlan been following the Grandfather? How long had he *almost* caught him? The City Watch had a name for that – dog trailing. And when you Dog Trailed someone for a really long time there was this thing the veterans talked about – this thing where you began to think you'd never catch him. It made your responses slower. Reduced your creativity.

Hey!

But Marielle had the advantage. She hadn't been dog trailing for long. She had to get to him before he took to those stairs. Her eyes were sweeping across the crowd, looking for an opening. She was moving before she was even certain, leaping up onto a passing hand cart and jumping from there over a knot of people carrying barrel staves and hammers. What had happened in this place?

No time to think of that.

Tamerlan could leap better than she could. And he had balance like a cat. She landed him on a balustrade at the top of the stairs, allowing him a single breath to catch himself before leaping again with all his strength.

The Grandfather's back was to them as he reached the head of the staircase. He wouldn't see them. There was no chance this time that he'd spiral away. She landed on his back like an angry cat, clawing for his throat through the thick purple scarf. It came loose, tangling around one of Tamerlan's wrists at the same time that his thumbs sank into the other man's windpipe and squeezed.

Don't kill him! He needs to be alive.

She wasn't going to kill him. She was going to subdue him. She'd seen Carnelian do this once. Even her name shot regret through Marielle, but she had no time for that now. With all her might, she pressed down as the Grandfather spun in her grasp, forcing her to adjust her grip, until his eyes met hers. There was no laughter in them now. His eyes rolled back until all she saw were the whites and he slumped heavily on the cobblestones.

Hurry! The crowd doesn't like this.

He was right about that. They were closing in, a growl already in their throats. With a worried sound, she hurriedly wrapped the scarf around the Grandfather's limp wrists, cinching it as tightly as the silk allowed and then threw him up over Tamerlan's thick shoulders.

How strong was he? He took the weight of the Grandfather as if it were no more than a sack of potatoes.

And now what? I might be able to carry him, but I'll struggle to fight like this.

Fight?

She looked around him and her eyes grew wide at the sight of a ring of revolutionaries – that was who they must be. None of them wore a uniform. Their clothing said dockworker, bouncer, tavern drunk, blacksmith's apprentice, librarian – she could go on. Dozens of careers represented and all with tools of the trade – hammers, barrel staves, cargo hooks, and truncheons – rather than usual weapons. But that didn't make them any less deadly.

"Is that a palace guard uniform I see on you, boy?" the tavern drunk called.

What was Tamerlan wearing? Marielle looked down to see the blue tabard that Etienne had given him so long ago. Uh oh. In a revolution, the only thing you didn't want to be was part of the old city structure.

"We're done with your kind here!"

They closed in around Tamerlan and the Grandfather and Marielle brought up the shell one more time. Would the echo be too faint? Could she still get enough magic to travel with it?

She blew gently. Nothing.

Blew again. Nothing.

A blow crashed into Tamerlan's lower back and she flinched, falling to one knee. The Grandfather felt suddenly too heavy. But they were so close! So close to having him finally in their grasp!

With all her might, she blew into the shell, thinking of how she used to hop through time and space without a problem before she took over Tamerlan. She could do it again. She could.

She just had to get them to the clock!

Sparks flew and they whirled in place. Purple and yellow. Yellow and purple.

It was working!

The cylinder of Spice dropped from Tamerlan's mouth.

And Marielle dropped from his mind like a heavy brick.

35: New Legend

Tamerlan

The sparks faded, leaving him gasping for breath with the unconscious Legend over his shoulders.

Marielle? Marielle?

She was gone. His mind felt dull and achy without her.

We're still here, pretty man.

Lila was no consolation. Not compared to Marielle.

If you like being commanded by a woman, then smoke again and I'll be here to hold your hand. I can do more than that hawk-nosed law-girl anyway.

He ignored her as the ground beneath him bucked and heaved. He was on a balcony somewhere and the railing shook back and forth, the rails rattling like dry bones as they rubbed against each other.

This place was fancy – a palace perhaps? Marielle had been trying to take him to H'yi – could this be the palace there? He didn't know if it had been burnt with everything else. But there was a tang to the air – a tang he wouldn't have noticed if he hadn't spent so much time with Marielle. Was that saltwater? Was he near the sea?

He pushed himself to his feet, wobbling under the weight of the Grandfather and stumbled toward the shaking railing.

This was not just a palace – this was the Great Hall in a palace. Like the Great Hall in the Seven Suns palace, this hall was not just massive but also full of curiosities. The wreck of a ship, carefully positioned on its side, cleaned, and fitted for an audience to sit within and still be able to see the hall, was on one side, a plaque near the bow to explain its origins. Was that Queen Mer's bust on the ship's head?

A waterfall fell from one of the other balconies, arranged over a series of rocks with statues of fish and squid worked between the falling water. It plunged into a pool below.

He didn't have time to note the fish skeletons, the coral, the strange art made of pearls – an eerie sight after witnessing the death of Mer's avatar – because in the center of the Hall was something far more captivating.

Were those leaders of the Retribution below?

They stood in a silent ring, blowing into shells – but these weren't little palm-sized shells. These were shells large enough to hold Tamerlan inside of them.

Look! They still have that?

What had King Abelmeyer so concerned?

Dragon. Ram sounded the same as always.

Queen Mer's Conch! Lila sounded awed. Strange – he didn't hear anything from Maid Chaos. She was gone now – gone forever.

Was anyone else missing? That was a chilling thought. Or was it? Would it really be so bad if more of them were gone?

If we're gone, then you have to figure out all of this on your own. Think you're ready for that, pretty man?

He wasn't. He didn't even know what they were doing down below.

You don't? Watch carefully.

Dragon. Dragon.

He leaned against the rail and looked down. It wasn't like he could creep out of here with an unconscious prisoner on his shoulders anyway.

The leaders of the Retribution – and that was definitely who they were! – were dressed in closely tailored coats with wide slashes cut in armpits and at the hips to allow movement. Their hair was cut short except for a long lock in the front. The length of the lock varied from one to another, suggesting rank of some kind. Each of their faces bore tattoos of different color in what looked like coastlines or maps. On one woman, it was a ragged shoreline drawn in burnt orange just under her eyes and across the bridge of her nose. Another had a light blue mountain range up her left cheek. Sepia trails split and crossed on the forehead of one of the men – a craggy, hard fellow with arms thicker than Tamerlan's. There were more – too many more for him to note them all, but it gave them a rakish look of born adventurers.

They blew into the massive conch shells which were arranged in a ring around one man – a man standing in a whale-bone cage. He stood still, almost calm, though his eyes were wild. Clothed only in a short pair of trousers, his bare skin was so full of tattoos swirling out of the windrose on his lower ribs, that there wasn't a bare patch left.

He seemed important.

He would have to be, Abelmeyer said. *Only the worthy are chosen as Legends.*

The ground heaved again, and a chunk of plaster fell from the ceiling, smashing on the floor beside the cage – yet no one stopped. The blowers kept blowing, their conches making a low, eerie sound, and the man in the cage didn't flinch. He was perfectly still despite his tortured eyes.

Do you see the north star between his eyebrows?

It was tattooed there in red.

It is the ancient sign of a Fleet Commander of Mer. If I were going to judge, I would guess this man led the fleet before this moment.

What were they going to do to him?

They're going to make him a Legend.

Tamerlan gasped. A Legend? What did Abelmeyer mean by that?

Dragon. Dragon. Dragon.

How do you think we became Legends, Tamerlan? We made a sacrifice for our city. We bound the dragons with our lives and blood. When the Grandfather destroyed Maid Chaos' avatar it woke the dragon Choan. And here we are, watching these people fix that. They will chain Choan again before he can rise and destroy the city.

The floor beneath him shook again, so hard this time that the balcony rippled under him like the waves of the ocean. Tamerlan clenched his teeth as they chattered in his head. There was nothing for it. He'd just have to keep trying to put the Grandfather back into the clock. Whatever madness this was could be dealt with later.

Do you think so? It's possible that very soon, there will be another voice in your head.

He shuddered. If only Marielle was still there. She'd held back his madness.

The man in the whalebone cage lifted up into the air, glowing faintly. His eyes rolled back into his head. A strange sound emerged from him – like a scream with his mouth still shut. What did it require to make a Legend?

A lot of things. But one of them is making the avatar – and no one survives that process.

They were going to kill him?

Worse. They're going to make him immortal.

No time for panic. No time for regrets. With a sigh, he shook himself.

If this was Choan, then out there somewhere were his friends in Jhinn's gondola. If he could get out of here – somehow – he could get to them.

Call on us! We will take you!

No. Better to do this himself. He hurried from the balcony, out into the passageway beyond.

He'd expected regular palace behavior – servants at work, Landholds strolling from place to place – or something. He hadn't expected chaos.

This was worse than Yan.

Screams and shrieks filled the air as people rushed through the passageways with baskets, or random items clutched to chests or trailing behind them on the ground. No one here was injured or caked in mud or oranges, but the undercurrent of fear and turmoil was as thick here as it had been in Yan or Xin – worse. And no wonder with the dragon bucking and heaving beneath them and the palace gave way with every roll – plaster falling in chunks from the ceiling, whole rooms buckling as their ceilings collapsed. Far from the calm in the Great Hall, these passageways were ruled by panic.

Women clutching small children to their breasts ran with wild eyes while men held anything close to a weapon that they could find – as if you could fight a dragon the size of a city – or even this disciplined army of invaders with curtain rods and ornamental spears. But what else could they do with their world falling apart? He knew what it was like to grasp at straws on a narrow hoe of saving a loved one.

No longer afraid of guards, Tamerlan plunged toward the outer walls of the palace. If he could find a way out to the canals – well, that would be a start. The Grandfather was getting heavy and his knees felt weak under him.

By the time he'd made his way to the outer walls, his arms and back were aching. Sweat poured down his forehead. No one had commented on his captive. No one had stopped him. No one had seemed to even care – though compared to the fallen rubble and broken pottery in the halls, compared to the bodies he'd seen collapsed or heaped in corners in the halls – people injured in the shaking or hurt in the stampedes of their fellow man – the unconscious man he carried was hardly unique.

He pushed through a narrow door to the outer palace wall. He was going to have to climb a flight of steps to reach the top of the wall and be able to look out. Could he manage that? His legs were like jelly under him – like the stems of wilted flowers. He wasn't going to make it.

He let his mind listen to the Legends. Maybe they would have a word of encouragement.

Smoke and we will help!

Would you get out of here?

It almost sounded like they were fighting. Their voices were strained and snappy.

Stop holding yourself back! Just call us over the Bridge!

Were they in pain?

He mounted the steps, struggling under the weight of the Grandfather. When he reached the top, the cacophony in his mind was so intense that he couldn't make out individual voices anymore. Everything was pain, pain, pain. His head was going to explode.

It felt too hard to look out across the city. It didn't help that the city seemed to roll and twitch as the dragon under it slowly woke. Pain made vision difficult. He blinked hard at the flowers of darkness that burst across his vision. Through the pain, he tried to find the canals, tried to trace them through fleeing people, battling groups, erupting fires.

If chaos had a name, it was Choan. If chaos had a homeland, it was the Dragonblood Plains.

Did he hear his name? It was hard to hear anything at all with his mind so full of screams, grunts, and shrieks.

In the distance, he saw the Fleet ships still creeping up the canals lighting everything they found on fire or sinking them beneath the murky water.

He stumbled forward, leaning against the lip of the wall, looking down into the moat.

He was seeing things. He was pretty sure of it. Stars of light burst between the flowers of darkness and between that and the confusion in his mind he didn't know what his own thoughts were. He wanted to see Jhinn in the moat below. Wanted it more than anything. So, of course, that was what he was seeing.

Up on the lip! Push the Grandfather over!

That didn't make sense, but it was the only clear thought he'd had in so long.

He pushed his burden over.

And then panic hit.

What had he done?

The man would drown, and it would be too late to rescue Marielle from the clock! This was madness!

He heard the splash of the Grandfather's body hitting the moat. At least he'd hit water and not stone.

He struggled up onto the top of the lip of the palace wall, shaking as the wall rolled and heaved under him, and then stumbled forward into an awkward fall.

Would he be able to find the Grandfather with his vision faltering and his hearing gone? Would he be able to keep him from drowning?

This was all his fault. What a fool thing to do! Dragon's blood in a cup, but he was a fool!

He hit the water hard, belly first, smacking his face and arms against the surface of the water. Everything stung as he fell below the thick, algae clumped water of the moat. His mouth was full of it, his nose, his ears. He couldn't see anything.

Something tugged at him as he tried to swim further down to find the Grandfather.

He was losing his mind.

He'd failed.

He'd failed and he was going insane.

And he was just so furious. He'd been so close and then one stupid thought and he'd lost everything he'd worked for. Fool! Fool! Fool!

If he died down here, he'd deserve it.

He was stuck on whatever was tugging at him. Stuck!

Something yanked him backward and warm air hit his face. He sucked in a breath before he hit something hard again.

"Stop fighting me, boy! Stop!"

He was so insane that now he was imagining Jhinn, wet and slimy with algae. Anglarok by his side frowning angrily with the sodden Grandfather in his arms.

Something was jammed between his lips.

"Here, do yourself a favor."

He pulled in a breath and the world began to spin.

36: Fight for Footing

Tamerlan

"Mer's spit in a cup! Depths take us all!" Liandari's cursing sounded both awed and horrified at once. "For the love of the brine, preserve us! For the love of the wind in sails, forfend!"

He blinked and his sight was clear again.

I'm here – for now.

Marielle! She stood him up so he could see. The whole gondola had moved with them – Jhinn, Liandari, Anglarok, Etienne and the Grandfather. They floated on the top of the water together. He hadn't been seeing things. Jhinn had been there just under the wall on the moat.

He's remarkably receptive to listening to requests from spirits. All I had to do was ask.

She'd brought him there to help. Marielle, that was genius!

But that wasn't all, was it? The world still tilted and rocked wildly under their gondola, but the buildings around them were not the white army-filled streets of Choan. The streets around them were empty – except for burnt-out husks of buildings. What had happened to Choan?

I learned the Grandfather's trick. This isn't Choan. I've brought you to me – to H'yi.

Tamerlan cleared his throat.

Hurry!

And then she was gone from his mind, pushed out by another spirit.

I'll take it from here, Deathless Pirate said, grabbing Tamerlan's body and shoving Jhinn aside to seize the oar and begin to steer the gondola in the wrong direction.

No! This was wrong! Wrong!

His companions were staring at him open-mouthed – all but Jhinn whose eyes had narrowed speculatively and Etienne who was frowning in judgment. They knew what was going on.

He's mine! Tamerlan stumbled as Lila took him over so forcefully that it was a wonder his mind was still in his own body. He leaned over the edge of the gondola and vomited, his belly upset from the sudden switch.

"He's finally gone mad," Liandari said, worry in her eyes. "We need to put him down like a dog."

"No!" That was Jhinn. "Give him a moment."

There was a shove again and then Lila was gone.

I can't hold them off for long! They want to have you. Hurry!

Marielle! She was fighting for him.

There had to be some way that he could fight, too. There had to be some way to stop being an innocent victim and start getting back some control.

I trust that you'll find a way, Tamerlan. Keep fighting!

Tamerlan dropped the oar like it was hot, holding his hands up.

"I just need to get the Grandfather into the clock," he said as the water beneath the gondola tipped, sending them speeding down the canal. The entire canal rose up and leaned toward the center of the city like a flowing river, spilling up over the shelf and into the streets which were usually high above the water. In the boat, everyone grabbed for something for support while Jhinn fought the current, grabbing the oar again, steering the gondola along the surge of water.

Liandari gripped the gunwales of the gondola with a fierce look in her eyes. "This dark magic ends now, Etienne. I don't know where you've brought us or why you did it so dramatically, but this ends now. The world is ending! Do you not see it heave and roll beneath us?"

"I didn't bring us here. And don't you know that beneath the city lies a dragon?" Etienne said, face pale. "It's waking."

"Dragon?" Anglarok said. His eyes were wide with fear, but he clenched his jaw powerfully, unwilling to give in to it. "Here, too?"

Tamerlan ignored them, reaching into the bottom of the boat to lift the Grandfather to his shoulders again. He could see the clock ahead and whether it was a dragon propelling them toward it or not, he knew what he needed to do. He felt with one hand for his knife – still there. He'd be ready.

"What do you think makes the city shake and roll?" Etienne asked. "The dragon is lifting from where he slept beneath H'yi. And no wonder. No one has been walking the mandala. The ancient pact our ancestors made with the Legends to keep the dragons down is gone now. He is rising into the air!"

It was never a pact, Marielle said in my mind. *It was forced on them. They were trapped into it. They didn't choose this selflessly. Or at least, not all of them.*

Who could force a Legend to do anything?

Who do you think? The unnamed one. The one who hates dragons with all his heart!

Was she saying that Ram the Hunter had trapped them as avatars to bind the dragons?

I love that you're quick. You keep up.

But he didn't have time to enjoy the compliment. They were nearly at the clock's base. Jhinn steered them roughly toward where the steps – mostly underwater now – led up to it from the canal.

"I'll try to stay here, but with these waves, I can't promise anything," he panted. He was holding the rail beside the steps, trying to keep the gondola against them as it bucked in the haphazard waves.

Tamerlan nodded and jumped up. He didn't look back as he ran up the stairs with the Grandfather in his arms. His leg muscles screamed with effort.

The ground bucked under him, forcing him to one knee. He bit his tongue in the jolt and tasted blood, but he struggled up again, forcing himself upward, each step an effort in determination.

Behind him, he heard Etienne demanding that he wait. "You don't have to do this alone!"

Marielle's presence vanished from his mind at the same moment that he was taken over again.

Deathless Pirate heaved the Grandfather off Tamerlan's shoulder, letting him fall heavily to the ground.

No! Not now! This timing was terrible!

"No one deserves to be caged!" Deathless Pirate drew Tamerlan's sword, spun and lunged toward Etienne, but a sharp pain stopped him in his tracks.

He roared in agony as pain flooded Tamerlan's mind. Deathless Pirate spun again to see Liandari pulling her sword back out of his thigh where blood poured down, soaking his leg. She'd come out of nowhere!

He leapt forward, but he was pulled back immediately, a thick forearm wrapping around his neck.

"I told you he was insane," Liandari said coolly, wiping her blade on the edge of Tamerlan's cloak as if he were a curtain or a rag. "I don't know why you associate yourself with him."

And just like that, Deathless Pirate was pulled away, flung out of Tamerlan's mind like an enemy tossed away by a great warrior. He reeled from it, sinking into Etienne who had him by the neck.

"Easy Tamerlan, easy!" Etienne hissed between clenched teeth. "Fight this back or I'll slit your throat myself!"

Was he seeing things, or had he actually seen Deathless Pirate pulled away and thrown back over the Bridge? Was he seeing him now as he fought Lila Cherrylocks, scrambling in unarmed combat with her like two drunks fighting in an alley? Or was he just going mad?

You see true. Chaos rules once more. And the dragons rise. Ram the Hunter's voice echoed through his mind.

"Get the old man," Liandari commanded as she bent to take the Grandfather's shoulders in her hands. Anglarok stooped for his feet.

"When you put the old man in the clock, you must be careful," Ram said with Tamerlan's voice. "And you must be quick."

"Shut him up," Liandari growled. "I don't take orders from the insane."

"Come on," Etienne said, pushing Tamerlan in front of him as they climbed the steps just behind the Harbingers. He was more gentle than Tamerlan had expected. "We started this thing together. Let's finish it."

Tamerlan felt ill. He could feel the other Legends tugging and pulling him even as Ram stayed in control of his body. He had to keep them at bay. He had to take control of himself. With all his might he pushed, sending everyone back over the Bridge. He was gasping for breath with the effort as they climbed step after step.

"If you ever touch that mixture again, I'll kill you myself." Etienne's voice as grim.

"It got us here, didn't it?" Tamerlan protested. What else could he have done? If there had been any other viable choices – any at all! – he would have taken them, but the only other choice would have been to give up. And Tamerlan wasn't the type to give up.

The ground rolled under them as they reached the street above, and it took all their concentration to keep their feet. There was no looking back. No time for it. No energy for it. Anglarok and Liandari struggled up the steps, carrying the Grandfather awkwardly between them.

What would they do to escape this city once Marielle was out of the clock? Would she still be able to hop people through time and space?

No time to worry about that. Ram shuddered as he tried to get back into Tamerlan's head. When he finally broke through, it was so sudden that Tamerlan's eyes widened with surprise.

"When you open the door to put the Grandfather in and take the girl out, it opens a wide door for the Legends," Ram said with his voice. "It's a trap for fools. But it is also a way out for anyone clever enough to jump from the other side. You must all stand clear of the clock – as far back as you can. Don't give them a way out! Make your minds tough! Concentrate on what you are doing and nothing else. Do you hear me? Nothing else!"

Liandari cursed and Anglarok shot him a worried look. They thought he was insane. But better that than to tell them the truth. After all, they were looking for the man who had opened the Bridge of Legends and if they knew that was him – well, they'd razed a city looking. If they'd do that to the people in their way, what would they do to the person who opened the Bridge?

They hurried up the last steps to the clock. Etienne's grip was still tight on Tamerlan's neck. The Grandfather was beginning to stir, babbling slightly as they reached the top of the steps.

He'd worked so hard to get here. He wanted to be here in person – not as an avatar for a Legend. He shoved mentally at Ram with all his might. The Legend fell away and Tamerlan stumbled in surprise. How had that worked?

Hurry! Ram said as he was flung from Tamerlan's mind.

Tamerlan had the strangest sensation of being able to see – though he saw nothing – and what he felt like he could see was a group of Legends charging the Bridge as Ram fought to defend it.

If he failed, Tamerlan would fight, too. He wouldn't be their plaything. Not now.

They reached the bottom of the clock to where the ghostly Marielle winked in and out of existence as the pendulum passed through her.

A tingling sensation washed over Tamerlan as he drew closer. They were finally here. After everything that had happened, they'd made it.

"Don't get sentimental on me now," Etienne growled, loosening his grip on Tamerlan. "Just spit some of that blood running down your chin on that door and open it up!"

Tamerlan blinked at his words. Oh yes, it needed his dragonblooded blood to open it.

He spat hard at the clock as they reached the door, his blood spattering across it in a grisly rainbow as Etienne reached for the latch and pulled the door open.

"Let me go now, Etienne," he asked calmly. "This is what I came here for."

Liandari and Anglarok grunted as they stood the Grandfather up waiting to put him into the clock.

"I smell – magic. Powerful magic and terrible things," Anglarok said in a pained voice.

But Tamerlan wasn't looking at that. He had eyes for only one. There she was.

Marielle.

She was perfect.

Absolutely perfect.

Tamerlan stepped forward, pulling free of Etienne at the sight of Marielle's delicate figure winking in and out of life. His eyes locked onto her, frozen in place – her lips slightly parted in surprise and one hand partially raised – inside the infinite time of timelessness. He'd drawn her face a thousand times. But he'd forgotten the exact turn of the corner of her mouth. He'd forgotten the dent in her chin that made his chest ache.

She was so beautiful – beautiful as the thousand upon a thousand sunrises seen by time, beautiful as an age of growing things, of calves birthed on mountains, of fish blooming in the wide sea. Her eyes held the sparkle of the ages, the light of life. She was hope. She was what he'd fought for, lost his mind for, given his soul for. She was everything.

Her beauty didn't lay in her tangled hair or tattered clothing – still streaked with mud and weeds from when the Grandfather kidnapped her. It didn't lay in her strong features or slightly crooked nose. It lay in her being Marielle – the one person who always saw true, who would do what was right no matter what it cost her, who would fight to the end for justice. It was a matchless beauty – unrivaled. Perfect.

He slipped past the Grandfather and the whispering Harbingers, and he stepped into the clock with her. It felt almost too personal – as if he'd stepped into her chambers when she was unaware – and he bit his lip apprehensively, careful with each movement.

He leaned in close, awed by her and careful, so careful. She'd been in here for so long. What toll would that take on a body?

Her lips were inches away as the ghostly pendulum swung through them both and he wanted so badly to meet them with his kiss. He ached so much to touch her that his skin tingled with wanting. His lips felt dry with needing to touch hers.

But that wouldn't be right. Not now. Not like this. Not without her permission.

Instead, he leaned in close, breathing in her breath. It was a caress of its own. A kiss without kissing. As if he could draw her in and keep her as close as he could keep her breath. He closed his eyes and let it fill him, savoring the moment.

Etienne grunted beside him, shattering the perfect shard of time.

"You can have special moments later. We have work to do now," he said roughly.

Tamerlan wrapped his arms gently around Marielle and delicately as a mother lifting a newborn, he lifted her up, drawing her from the clock as he stepped backward.

In his mind, chaos bloomed as the Legends fought and gnashed against his determination to hold them back, but in his heart were order and peace as he took her from the clock, stepping out onto the street. Her eyes were closed and a white wisp – like a spiderweb but wide as a ribbon – stretched between her and the pendulum.

The Harbingers shoved the Grandfather roughly into the clock the moment he left it and leapt backward as Etienne sliced the cord of spiderweb with his belt knife.

But they didn't close the door of the clock.

And as Marielle's eyes flickered open and the color returned to her cheeks, a roar filled the air.

37: Close the Clock

Marielle

She woke in his arms and the smell of him filled her up like a festival meal. Honey and cinnamon and the scent of tarragon swirled through the air in clouds of gold, almost overwhelming the scent of all the magic that was already making her head spin with its lilac scent and turquoise colors mixed with gold sparks. Her eyes fluttered open and she saw him there, like a tortured saint, like a dying man clinging to a last scrap of wood.

There was no Legend controlling him. He was just himself – beautiful, guilt-ridden, desperate, and sensitive. His eye was dark and haunted again. Ever since she'd met him, his eyes had only grown darker with the burdens he carried. She wanted to tell him it would be better. She wanted to soothe away his pain and rub the wrinkles out of his forehead.

Something roared behind him like a powerful wind. He straightened and she gasped.

Behind him, through the door of the clock – white wisps clawed out like the reaching arms of tentacles. One snatched up Liandari, whipping her into the air.

Marielle leapt from Tamerlan's arms.

"The clock!" she called over the wind. "Close the door! You have to close it!"

She rushed toward the clock, but she could already scent the magic pouring out of it in all its lilac and turquoise intensity. Tamerlan rushed in beside her, shoving the door as hard as he could. She felt Etienne before she saw him – smelled his dark intensity – orange with the overwhelming scent of cloves – as strongly as if he was spewing magic out, too. Together, they pushed at the door of the clock.

It closed an inch. Another inch. But something was holding it.

She turned her head. Anglarok was gripping Liandari with both fists, screaming as the tentacle of white magic throttled her. It was that tentacle that was holding the door – and it was those tentacles that they had to stop.

If this really was a trap – a trap for Legends, then they needed to get it shut before it could trap Liandari, too. If only she could remember what she'd heard Ram saying before she'd left the clock. Something about traps.

She let go of the door and leaned across Tamerlan to draw his sword from his scabbard. Maybe if she cut it the way Etienne had cut the cord that held her. She raised the sword and hacked at the white band of spirit as hard as she could. If it made a difference, she didn't see it.

"Close it with blood," Etienne gasped. "Put your leg against it, Tamerlan."

Sweat ran down his face. All his might was being thrown into the door. So was Tamerlan's. He grunted, but when he shifted his stance, the door slipped back a span.

"Let me," Marielle said, sliding her hand down his leg to bloody her palm on his wound. He shuddered at her touch. That wound would need tending. It pained her to take from him again. She was always taking – his body, his blade, and now his blood. She shook her head as she wiped her hand on the door. She owed him better than always taking.

The door of the clock slammed shut with the boom of a sepulcher.

"Liandari! Lieutenant!" Anglarok's voice sounded panicked.

She spun to see him frozen with his leader in his arms. She lay limp in his grasp, but the tentacle was gone. Her face was white as snow, but her eyes flickered open.

He should have smelled it first. Maybe he was too concerned for her. Maybe it was hope that blinded him.

"Watch out!" Marielle cried as the scent whipsawed through her nose.

Legend! The smell of magic mixed with insanity was clear as a bell being struck. She'd smelled this before. She smelled it every time Tamerlan was possessed. She smelled it every time that she'd fought the Legends for him.

She held out Tamerlan's blade but the world beneath them rocked wildly, shaking them so that they stumbled and had to focus on their footing. And then a shadow blocked the sun and as she looked up, her belly seemed to drop within her as a massive head – a dragon head – curled up and over the city.

It looked down at the clock positioned between its wings like a man might look at a dagger in his back. The blackened ruins of the city opened up, houses and roads falling from them like scales from a dead fish, and a red eye glared at Marielle at the same moment that Liandari leapt to her feet and out of Anglarok's grasp.

"Dragon!" she cried, taking off at a sprint toward the University District.

Toward the head.

"Liandari!" Anglarok called. He sprinted forward but was flung off his feet by another lurch from underneath them. What was left of the masonry of the nearby buildings fell in chunks around them.

Tamerlan reached out to help Anglarok up on his feet.

"She's possessed," he breathed in horror.

There was something wrong with the sun, Marielle realized. Something wrong with where it was on the horizon.

"Possessed by *what?*" Anglarok asked through chattering teeth.

"I think," Etienne paused to cough or maybe choke. "I think that perhaps the dragon we are standing on is flying now. Are those mountains closer than they were a moment ago?"

He was right. The mountains were closer.

The sun hadn't moved.

They had.

"Possessed by a Legend," Tamerlan said to Anglarok and at his look of horror, he continued. "Ram the Hunter, if I had to guess – though it could easily be one of the others."

"Mer preserve us!" Anglarok said and his hands shook as they moved to cover his mouth. "That means that we opened it. We opened the Bridge of Legends!"

Tamerlan and Etienne exchanged a guilty look.

And Marielle knew why. It wasn't Liandari who had opened the Bridge – or at least, not the first time.

"Mountains fall on us! World swallow us up!" Anglarok screamed, looking up at the sky as the dragon screamed, too – a piercing sound like a gull crying along the shore. "We have opened death! We have brought our own destruction on our heads!"

"Now, who is crazy?" Tamerlan muttered. But his hands were compassionate when he took Anglarok by the arm and led him to the edge of the steps to help him sit.

"Take a moment. Take a breath. We'll go after her in a moment.

"There's no point going after her until the city lands somewhere," Etienne said, trying to keep his feet under him as the city rolled again beneath them.

"She could be gone by then," Tamerlan said calmly. "And who knows what she might do with a Legend possessing her."

"*You* would know," Etienne said grimly. "So tell me, Legend Boy – where will she go? What will she do?"

Queasiness washed over Marielle. With the immediate urgency of leaving the clock past, her body was calling in debts one at a time. Her scent and vision wavered, and her legs trembled beneath her. Hunger roared through her like a hurricane. Whatever magic had sustained her through her months in the clock was gone and with it, her strength.

Tamerlan noticed. He reached for her with a kind smile and eased her into a seated position beside Anglarok. Tamerlan's leg was still bleeding. Little pools kept forming around his foot.

"Let me tend that," she said, fighting the urge to vomit as she felt his injured leg.

"Thank you." Who thought a word could be so full? But from him, it spoke a thousand things at once. Things implied by his smile, but the glint in his blue eyes and by the fact that he was here – here saving her instead of anywhere else.

But after that brief smile, he turned to Etienne. "It looked like she was going after the dragon. So that means the palace, right? The one place where there's a chink in its armor."

Etienne nodded grimly.

"We have to go after her," Anglarok said, head in his hands. His voice sounded strange.

"Of course," Tamerlan agreed.

"Wait!" She tore his trousers around the wound. "This is bad. A sword cut. Who cut you?"

"Someone who was trying to help," he said mildly, his eyes lingering on her as if just watching her could give him something. She felt her cheeks growing hot under that gaze. It felt more than personal. It felt like she was his salvation. Again, he ripped his gaze away from hers. "And now we need to help her. The leg will have to wait."

"Don't you want the dragon dead?" Etienne asked with a look that suggested he was weighing Tamerlan and finding him wanting.

"Of course."

"Not until this is stitched," Marielle interrupted. Her head hurt and she felt like she might vomit, but he was bleeding worse than he thought he was. She wasn't going to let him bleed to death while he tried to heal the world.

"Then why go after her?" Etienne demanded as Marielle opened her belt pouch and took out the needle and thread she kept there. It was clear he wasn't going to wait. Maybe if she hurried, he'd at least let her stitch it.

Tamerlan looked haunted as he answered Etienne. "She isn't herself. And I don't want her to have to pay the price of being an avatar for a Legend. She's no friend of mine, but no one deserves that."

They nodded together and Etienne held out a hand. "Agreed."

Marielle stabbed the needle into Tamerlan's leg and started to stitch as he took Etienne's hand. He barely flinched as she worked. He really was crazy. And tough as an ox.

"We'll need a way to hold her once we get to her – and if there's a way to destroy this dragon, we should take it, too," Tamerlan said. "And we have to find Jhinn."

He shivered and Marielle felt a shared burst of horror. If the dragon was in the air, would there be any water left in the whole city?

"How long do you think Liandari will be possessed for?" Etienne asked. The ground still shook under them. It was a wonder that the two men could stay standing with the very city under their feet swaying as the dragon flew. The sound of falling masonry and crumbling buildings made talking over it a chore.

Tamerlan shook his head. "This is different than … well, you know how different it can be."

They were both silent, looking in the direction that Liandari had disappeared.

It wasn't until she was almost done stitching that Marielle realized Anglarok was gone.

"Where's Anglarok?" she asked as she finished the last stitch in Tamerlan's leg.

She looked over at where the other Scenter had been. He wasn't there. Somewhere in the distraction and noise, he had slipped away, leaving a single word written on the stone in blood – scrawled messily as if the owner of the finger that wrote it had been wrestling for control of his own hand.

It read "help."

Marielle felt the blood drain from her face as she met Tamerlan's working eye.

"Did the swath of magic touch him, too?"

Tamerlan shook his head – not a denial, simply confusion.

"I don't know," Etienne gasped.

Marielle swallowed as she put the thread and needle away and found her weary feet. "The Legends were determined to find new avatars and to do what they'd always hoped for – live again in this world. I think they've found two new avatars."

"We'll just wait until it wears off," Etienne said sensibly. "And then, Tamerlan, you will destroy every scrap of that Spice you have, do you understand?"

Marielle swallowed, but it was Tamerlan who spoke first.

"They didn't smoke," he said, turning in a circle to look in every direction as if he was searching for Anglarok.

"What?" Etienne's voice as all edge.

"They didn't smoke. This isn't temporary. Don't you see? I think that one of them – or maybe both – is permanently possessed by a Legend."

"And what does that mean?" Etienne asked.

"It means the Five Cities of the Dragonblood Plains are doomed," Marielle said. "It took everything Ram had to quell the Legends – every trick he could find. And if they're out there now, it will take every trick we can find, too."

EPILOGUE

TAMERLAN

They'd found clean clothing for Marielle and dried meats in one of the buildings that was still intact. It wouldn't be enough to help them for long. Wherever the dragon was headed, it was a place colder than the Five Cities. Already, they clutched cloaks around them against the cold as he flew ever onward and the day bled into the dark.

Jhinn had not been where they left him and there was no water in the canal when they checked. That alone had left them grim faced.

"We could set up camp," Etienne suggested halfheartedly when night fell, but no one bothered to reply. There was nowhere safe to stand still. Every one of them had survived a close call with falling buildings or been swept off their feet by a sudden movement from the dragon beneath them.

Crossing the city was harder than they'd imagined it would be. And when they finally reached their destination, there would be two Legends to fight. Tamerlan touched his oilcloth quently to check it was still there. There were six rolls in ere – or there should be. Six left. Would it be enough?

will be.

ne thing was certain. Neither of the Legends that had taken e Harbingers was Ram the Hunter.

rapped them once. I can trap them again. But first, we hunt dragons.

e reached out and took Marielle's hand, desperately grateful nen she let him. He needed to remember why he'd fought so rd to open up that clock – especially now that there were ice as many Legends free because of his choice.

wice as many Legends to dance havoc across the ragonblood Plains. Twice as many Legends to destroy erything.

BEHIND THE SCENES:

USA Today bestselling author, Sarah K. L. Wilson loves spinning a yarn and if it paints a magical new world, twists something old into something reborn, or makes your heart pound with excitement ... all the better! Sarah hails from the rocky Canadian Shield in Northern Ontario - learning patience and tenacity from the long months of icy cold - where she lives with her husband and two small boys. You might find her building fires in her woodstove and wishing she had a dragon handy to light them for her

Sarah would like to thank **Harold Trammel** and **Eugenia Kollia** for their incredible work in beta reading and proofreading this book. Without their big hearts and passion for stories, this book would not be the same.

Sarah has the deepest regard for the talent of her phenomenal artists – **Francesca Baerald** who designed the gorgeous map for this series and Lius Lasahido and his team at **Polar Engine** who created the gorgeous cover art that accompanies this book. Without their work, it would be so much harder to show off this story the way it deserves!

www.sarahklwilson.com

www.ingramcontent.com/pod-product-compliance
Lightning Source LLC
Chambersburg PA
CBHW051732020826
48982CB00015BA/491

* 9 7 8 0 9 8 7 8 5 0 2 9 4 *